THE WORMLING IV

The Minions of Time

THE WORMLING
BOOK IV

The Minions of Time

JERRY B. JENKINS
CHRIS FABRY

Tyndale House Publishers, Inc., Carol Stream, Illinois

Visit Tyndale's exciting Web site for kids at cool2read.com

Also see the Web site for adults at tyndale.com

TYNDALE and Tyndale's quill logo are registered trademarks of Tyndale House Publishers, Inc.

The Wormling IV: The Minions of Time

Designed by Ron Kaufmann

Edited by Lorie Popp

Published in association with the literary agency of Alive Communications, Inc., 7680 Goddard Street, Suite 200, Colorado Springs, CO 80920.

Library of Congress Cataloging-in-Publication Data

Jenkins, Jerry B.
    The Wormling IV : minions of time. / Jerry B. Jenkins, Chris Fabry.
        p. cm.
    Summary: Having discovered that he is the King's Son, Owen contemplates his future with trepidation as he must fulfill his destiny to lead the battle with the Dragon, unite the worlds of the Highlands and the Lowlands, and marry a princess.
    ISBN-13: 978-1-4143-0158-7 (sc)
    ISBN-10: 1-4143-0158-8 (sc)
    [1. Adventure and adventurers—Fiction.   2. Identity—Fiction.   3. Good and evil—Fiction.   4. Fantasy.]   I. Fabry, Chris, date.   II. Title.   III. Wormling four. IV. Title: Minions of time.
    PZ7.J4138Wou 2008
    [Fic]—dc22   2007030032

Printed in the United States of America

14   13   12   11   10   09   08
 7   6   5   4   3   2   1

For Jeremy

"You are as young as your faith, as old as your doubt;

as young as your self confidence, as old as your fear;

as young as your hope, as old as your despair."

GENERAL DOUGLAS MACARTHUR

✦

"To hope is to risk despair,

to try is to risk failure.

But risks must be taken because the greatest

hazard in life is to risk nothing. . . .

Only a person who risks is free."

WILLIAM ARTHUR WARD

✦

"It does not do to leave a live dragon out of your calculations,

if you live near him."

J. R. R. TOLKIEN

The greatest fear of the human heart is not a monster under your bed or losing all your money or being left stranded in a foreign country or being eaten by snakes or drowning.

Do not misunderstand—those are all dreadful predicaments. But be sure of this: the greatest fear of the human heart runs much deeper than these. Our greatest fear concerns who we really are. In that search for truth about our souls, we are most afraid of discovering not that we are nothing but that there is something wonderful and glorious about us. Something regal and noble and majestic. Something amazing.

If we are nothing, if we simply crawled upon the shore of human existence and stretched our fins until fingers appeared, no expectation of goodness rests upon us. We can simply live as we please, make decisions based upon the wants of our stomachs or our minds. We live and we die with no purpose other than to satisfy our cravings.

However—and let us pause here to mention what a wonderful word *however* is—if we were instead placed here, our lives have purpose and meaning. We do not have to make that up, for it is given to us by the someone who placed us here.

By chance, we are nothing. By design, our lives connect to each other and to the one who made us.

It was to these thoughts that our hero, Owen Reeder, put his mind. Small Owen—of low estate, the son of a bookstore owner, once perusing pages daily—has been thrust into a search for royalty and found it in himself. In reading *The Book of the King*, Owen discovered that he had been chosen to be a Wormling, entrusted with not only the book but also a special worm named Mucker, who was the transport between the Highlands (earth) and the Lowlands—a place Owen did not even know existed.

It is above these Lowlands that Owen currently flies, locked in a cage borne by a winged beast who smells vile and seems to have unending stamina. Other flyers are far ahead, Owen's group taking up the rear of the prisoner train.

And it is in this cage that Owen ponders his own station: namely, that he is the King's Son, the very one he had been searching for since first he arrived.

To say this frightened him would be the same as saying that falling a thousand feet onto concrete would hurt. Owen was terrified. He couldn't comprehend all this. What would it mean for his family, his mission, his destiny?

The Book of the King said the Son would lead forces to battle the Dragon. He would help unite the two worlds—the Highlands and Lowlands. But chief among Owen's concerns was that he was also prophesied to wed the princess Onora. He had never held a girl's hand, let alone kissed one—not that he hadn't thought about it.

Owen had learned that along with great fear comes a certain comfort. If all he had discovered was really true, he had a history. He had a family. Not just a father but also a mother who loved him. A sister who had been taken captive. And a bride waiting.

Not comforting was the prospect of the Dragon's talons sinking into his chest, not to mention the beast's thousands upon thousands of followers who would comprise a gigantic force against him.

Such is curious about despair: each time comfort seeped into Owen's soul, the thought of the enemy and the task soon overwhelmed him. He had seen the Dragon up close, but that was as the Wormling, a seeker, an ant scurrying from the foot-steps of giants. Now Owen knew he was this beast's mortal enemy.

All this thinking was, of course, moot—pointless. Owen was high above the ground, smushed into the corner of a cage with people from the Castle on the Moor, including the king of the west. Most of these were servants trying in vain to keep their soiled garments from touching the king and queen. The people treated Owen as less than human, sneering and jeer-ing at him for speaking to some unseen visitor. They thought he had been talking to himself, studying the underside of the great flying beast.

A child yelled, getting everyone's attention and pointing to water over the horizon, waves against the shore, and beyond that, an island.

Owen sat thinking of his friends Watcher and Humphrey. He'd told them to meet him in a secret place, and he imag-ined them waiting, pacing, wondering.

Owen suddenly sat up. The island looked familiar. There was more than one. Yes, it was true. The islands of Mirantha. He had been here before—he had met Mordecai, a man still on the island as far as Owen knew. He picked up a pebble and threw it as hard as he could at the flying animal, trying to get it to change direction and fly toward the island.

"What are you doing?" a young boy said. "He can't even feel that."

Another prisoner yelled, "There's someone on that rock!"

They were flying along the path Owen and Watcher had taken to Erol's clan. Huge rock formations loomed, and as the creature passed close to them, a lone figure stood on a precipice eyeing them.

Erol! Owen stood and shouted and waved.

"What do you think he's going to do?" an older woman said. "Rescue you? From down there? You're crazy."

Owen kept yelling. As they drew nearer, several others from Erol's group climbed out on top of the rocks.

"Are these friends of yours?" a man wearing the king's coat of arms said.

"Very good friends," Owen said.

"Then you might want to call off their archers. They're amassing on the ledge. If they bring this beast down, we'll all be killed."

A dozen of Erol's men had bows drawn and at the ready. The beast seemed not to notice and flew straight for the rock.

"Erol! It's me! The Wormling! Lower your weapons! Don't shoot!"

But the leader raised an arm and dropped it. Arrows flew.

"Get down!" Coat of Arms yelled. "Everybody on the floor!"

The arrows overflew the cage, and some lodged in the

animal's neck. One hit him in the mouth and stuck through a lip. The rest pierced his wings and passed through. The beast swerved toward the rocks, scattering Erol and his men.

"Hang on!" Coat of Arms hollered.

The cage smacked the top of a rock, sending people flying around inside. Owen grabbed the bars and held on as the flyer listed left, then right. Blood trickled from a wound in the animal's neck.

Erol gave the fire signal again.

"No!" Owen shouted, but arrows whistled through the air and pierced the leathery skin with a *pfft*.

The flyer dipped toward a large rock, and at the last second Owen grabbed the young boy who had alerted them and pulled him close as the cage crashed again. The group pitched like toys in a box, banging the front of the cage as the flyer recovered and haltingly changed direction.

"Erol!" Owen screamed. "Help us!"

The archers grew tiny in the distance as the beast continued. Owen could tell it was laboring, its breathing erratic. Blood coursed from the wounds.

As they slowly descended, Coat of Arms rose from the floor and hobbled to the front, inspecting the bars. He pulled, but they were too strong. "There's room enough for the young ones to crawl through," he said.

"They'll die from the fall," a woman shrieked.

"It's their only chance!"

Several rushed to the front, and Owen gasped. No one else saw what lay ahead of them, and he could only hope the flyer had enough energy left not to crash.

Given the choice between crashing full force into a rock or water, Owen would have chosen the obvious. But he had been in these waters before and knew the Kerrol—a slimy, underwater beast that ate anything in its path—lived here. Owen and Watcher had barely escaped its clutches.

The flying beast was losing steam as it passed over the sandy beach. Wobbling and diving, then pulling up, it was like a roller-coaster ride with no rails. Women screamed and men turned white.

The king of the west struggled to gain his footing, and Owen moved closer. "Thank you for helping me back at the castle."

"Why didn't you use the horse and get away?" the king said as the cage splashed into the water, then shot back into the air.

"I wanted to help you."

"You fool! Now you'll die with us."

"Perhaps," Owen said. "But there may be a way out of this."

A young girl screamed and pointed at the water, where a long, slithering body passed in an arc.

"Does anyone have jargid skins?" Owen yelled.

"Who do you think you are?" Coat of Arms said. "Get away from the king!"

"Hurry!" Owen said.

"I have a skin," a maid said, pulling off her hat.

"I do as well," a man said, tossing one from his back toward Owen, who stuffed them into his shirt and hung on.

With a last gasp, the flyer tried to flap and lift. The force of the wind on the arrow holes in the animal's wings made them stretch, and the creature gave a high-pitched shriek and a mournful cry that echoed off the islands.

"He calls to the Dragon," Coat of Arms said.

"It is his last call," the king said.

A wing collapsed in on itself with a sickening crunch, and the creature began a whirling free fall toward the water. The prisoner-filled basket lurched.

"Perhaps the beast will float!" Owen yelled. "Or the bottom of the cage will!"

"Brace yourselves!" the king shouted.

Spiraling, winding, and weaving, the creature's back hit the water first, its wings tucked behind it, a wave engulfing it.

The flyer wobbled in the water, flailing, scratching, and clawing at the cage until it had a firm grip.

"Does anyone have a knife?" Owen said.

"They took our weapons."

People dangled through the bars, feet and arms in the water, grasping for footing, splashing, sucking in the salty liquid. Owen landed on top of the pile, three deep, and he sprang up, clothes and hair wet, grabbing the cage and hanging on. They were trapped.

The cage tipped left and came to rest on the creature's outstretched wing, floating on the surface as thin as a kite. The people clapped and smiled.

"Try to get the cage tipped over," the king said. "It will float, and the tide will take us to shore."

But the flyer gurgled and descended into the dark water, pulling the cage after it.

It is like children to spot something unusual, something askew on the horizon. And while everyone else in the cage was staring into the brack- ish depths, the young boy who had pointed out the water in the first place stared at Owen. His face was not filled with fear, like everyone else's, but as a child will focus on a flower while others move toward a picnic, this boy seemed enamored with Owen's appearance.

As they plunged beneath the sur- face, the child could not, of course, hold this stare, for by the way he thrashed and clawed, the fear of being trapped surely overtook him as well. They weren't just sinking; they were also descending at a rapid pace—dragged by something.

Owen held his breath, staring into the murky darkness. The speed threw people back toward him, and he had to move them out of the way to reach the front of the cage, desperately feeling for mangled bars until he could pull himself through.

The descent stopped suddenly. Owen quickly found the top of the cage and grabbed the leather bindings securing the flyer to the hitch. He discovered slack in the leather and pulled with all his might.

Bubbles gushed, and people fought to hold their breath. Owen felt something pass him and instinctively closed his eyes, remembering Mordecai's training. The man had made him catch fish blindfolded, sensing movement in the water with only his hands. "Become part of the world you are in," he had said. "Immerse yourself in every movement and molecule, and you will discover what you seek."

They had been underwater more than half a minute when Owen sensed movement to his left. A tail? A decoy? He quickly turned right and held out the leather bands as far as he could, clenching his teeth.

He peeked to find a pair of piercing, reptilian eyes on him. Jagged, sharp teeth lunged, and Owen let go of the bands. He darted down, grabbing onto the cage, now a whirlwind as the Kerrol finally chewed through the bands.

When the cage released, the Kerrol rose slightly in the stirring water. Owen swam underneath and pushed the cage toward the dim light of the surface.

Objects in water are always lighter due to the buoyancy, of course, but raising a cage full of people required more strength than Owen had. Something else was at work here. Someone else.

Owen's lungs were bursting, but he dared not gasp underwater. And if he felt this way, what of the people inside the cage? And the children? Had they already taken the deadly water into their lungs?

When the cage finally broke the surface with a great splash, Owen scrambled atop it, gasping, as heads, lips, and noses popped out through the bars to do the same. He jostled the bobbing cage up as far as he could, but there was only enough room for the people to get their heads out. Were they all there?

"Help the younger ones out!" Coat of Arms said. "At least save them!"

The people gasped and whimpered, splashing. Owen knew this would attract the Kerrol.

"Stay where you are!" Owen said. "I'll get you out!"

But how?

4
Whirlpool

Indecision often makes the difference between life and death. Owen had to act immediately, especially when he espied a small craft in the distance. Owen waved frantically. "Over here! Help!"

But then he felt water swirl beneath him again and had to dive and push the cage up far enough so the people could get air. All the splashing and screaming and choking had attracted their enemy. Owen floated under the cage, waiting, gauging his timing until the last second when the fierce beast appeared.

Owen pushed away, pulling his feet to his chest and just eluding the

Kerrol's teeth as its nose slammed the cage bottom. The cage burst free of the water, leaving in its wake a swirling mass of bubbles and brine and seaweed.

Owen surfaced to take a breath and saw the cage a few yards away, the bottom cracked in two, people scurrying to get out, and no Kerrol in sight. Owen's heart sank, knowing the Kerrol would grab them one by one as they tried to swim away.

He dived again, thrashing and screaming to attract the Kerrol. He resurfaced, splashing as violently as he could. The skiff was closer now, and those who could swim struggled toward it. Others held on to the cage, shuddering, whimpering for help.

Suddenly the Kerrol rose between the skiff and the escapees and opened wide, showing its knifelike teeth. Its roar sent shock waves across the water, and the people froze.

But Owen yelled and waved. "Hey, Kerrol, over here! Come on, you overgrown snake! Come and get me!"

The Kerrol turned and narrowed its eyes at Owen, nostrils flared. It dived for the depths, causing a wave to overtake the swimmers.

"Get to that skiff!" Owen yelled as the grateful swimmers screamed their thank-yous and flailed toward the craft.

"Ho there!" came the call of a familiar voice.

"Mordecai?" And as the water swirled and sucked Owen

down as if a plug had been pulled from a drain, he cried out, "Get them aboard, Mordecai!"

Foam and froth bubbled while Owen spun as if in a washing machine. The Kerrol was swimming in a circle below, causing the swirl. Owen slid down the funnel with his hand out, like a surfer touching the inside of a wave, unable to slow himself, pulled inexorably downward.

♦♦♦

At the bottom, the Kerrol prepared for his meal, lying in wait as the boy tumbled toward his gaping mouth.

5

On the Skiff

Mordecai helped the soggy people onto his boat. They sputtered and coughed, and some retched over the side, throwing up salt water.

"We must retrieve the king and queen," a fancily dressed man said, motioning at what was left of the cage.

Three children and a man and a woman dressed in finery clung to it.

"King of what?" Mordecai demanded.

"King of the west, sir," a woman said. "And we are his servants."

Mordecai sneered. "He's too close to the whirlpool."

"You cannot leave them," the man said.

"You left him. Why don't you go fetch him?"

"But the children," a woman pleaded. "We can't leave them."

"If that beast comes back, none of us will survive." Mordecai gave pieces of wood to the people and commanded them to row. He pulled a coil of vines from under a sack on the other side of the skiff.

With a mighty toss, Mordecai threw the vine near the cage. "Ho there! Grab this!"

The king and queen grabbed the vine, but the children would not follow. No matter what Mordecai or the others said, the three clung to the sinking cage.

Mordecai began to pull the vine, but as he did, the king let go and swam back to the cage. His wife grabbed for him, tugging at his robe, but he tore away and made it to the cage, prying the screaming children's hands from the bars. With the children on his back, he swam to the vine.

"Row!" Mordecai yelled as he pulled at the vine.

The people used the wooden slats to propel the vessel toward the islands.

When Mordecai had pulled the king, queen, and children to within 10 yards of the skiff, he said to the finely dressed man, "Who was that who yelled at me and dived in the water?"

"Just a boy," the man said. "He came to us shortly before the Dragon burned the castle."

"The Dragon?" Mordecai said. "And you say he came to you just before . . ."

The king pushed his wife onto the skiff and helped the children up. "He pretended to be someone else to the Dragon. He tried to save us."

Mordecai's heart quickened as he grasped the man's hand and pulled him aboard. "Describe him to me."

The world seemed to spin in a different direction. Not a day had gone by that Mordecai hadn't thought of his young friend. Not a day had gone by that he didn't regret letting him go. How had he fared in his quest for the Son? Had he been able to retrieve *The Book of the King*? That he had met the Dragon and lived was a good sign, but now . . .

Mordecai whispered, "The Wormling." He turned to those paddling and shouted, "Turn us around. Now!"

"You'll kill us all," the man in the fine coat said, nearly falling overboard. "We're overloaded as it is. Besides, that creature is sure to have—"

Mordecai grabbed the man and knotted his embroidered cloth with a fist. With clenched teeth and eyes that bored into the man, he said, "Do you know who he is? Do you know what he's trying to do? You do not deserve to be helped by someone like the Wormling."

The other passengers murmured among themselves. It was

clear they had heard of the Wormling and perhaps had been told tall tales about him.

"We didn't know, sir," a child said. "I thought there was something strange about his eyes, but I never dreamed he was the Wormling."

Mordecai switched the sail to turn the skiff toward the swirling water.

"I command you to turn this boat toward the island," the queen said. "You are subject to our rule."

"I am no more your subject than the wind is, madam," Mordecai said. "If you want to make for the island, start swimming. Otherwise keep your mouth closed."

Belly of the Beast

Sliding down the whirlpool toward the Kerrol, Owen realized it didn't matter how royal his blood was—he was about to be eaten. His best course was to tuck his arms to his sides and become a missile, hurtling past the teeth and slamming the back of the beast's throat with a thud.

Everything grew dark, and Owen felt the tongue of the creature try to push him toward the teeth. Owen grabbed the spiny tissue hanging above him—what is called an epiglottis in humans—and hung there a second before sliding down the Kerrol's throat.

♦♦♦

What a pity, the Kerrol thought. *Gone before I could chew you.*

Upset Stomach

Mordecai watched in horror as
the swirling stopped, the hole
closed, and the surface of the water
calmed. The people seemed to stare
in disbelief. All sounds from the
Wormling had ended, and the skiff lay
drifting lazily in open water. A black
gull passed overhead, then darted for
shore.

Mordecai studied the island with
dread before turning to his refugees.
"If you have any strength left, row for
your lives away from the island to the
other shore."

All but the king and the queen,
who had positioned themselves in the
middle of the skiff beside the sail pole,

stuck hands and wood in the water and worked. Even the children must have caught the fear in Mordecai's voice, for they leaned over the edge, trying to propel the skiff faster.

If the Kerrol had killed the Wormling, Mordecai only hoped it would be satisfied and not return to the surface. But who was he kidding? When had the Kerrol ever been satisfied? Mordecai had watched this beast devour sea and land creatures at will, and nothing ever stopped it. Only the Wormling had ever escaped it, and then only once. The Kerrol was an eating machine.

The lad had given his life for these people, and if Mordecai understood correctly, he hardly knew them. And what a way to die. At the bottom of a funnel of water, chomped by a hungry beast.

The skiff jerked violently forward, forcing Mordecai to wobble and ride it like a surfboard. And there, rising from the depths, came the huge serpent that had caused the wave. Mordecai slowly ran his gaze across the scaly skin to the monstrous head, vicious and feral, with dead, hungry eyes.

The people gasped. Although he had seen the monster many times, Mordecai had never been this close. It merely stared at the skiff, as if admiring a perfect plate of hors d'oeuvres. And Mordecai knew, as the largest man aboard, that he was the main course.

He stepped between the king and queen, quickly removed

the crudely made cloth sail, and pulled the pole from its holder. He wrestled it to his shoulder, causing those around him to duck, the sharp end of the pole aimed at the monster.

"You don't think you can kill that thing," the fancily dressed man said.

"Trying is better than not. I surely don't aim to go down without a fight."

"Reason with it!" the queen screeched.

"There is no reasoning with evil," Mordecai said, eyes locked on the monster. "I learned that long ago, and you'd best learn it as well."

Strangely, with the beast looming, other than the lapping water, all was silent. Mordecai knew how swift this creature was, and if it lunged, he planned to shove the pole directly into one of its eyes. It was their only hope.

But the Kerrol's seemingly puzzled eyes shifted. Its neck straightened, its throat bulged, and the green, scaly cheeks puffed like a child's mouth stuffed with sweets. It violently shook left, then right, finally snapping its head forward, then again only harder. The roiling water sent the skiff forward before the third lunge.

Mordecai dropped his jaw as something came hurtling from the creature's throat and shot from its mouth.

Forgive us if you're trying to eat whilst reading this, but we feel compelled to relate the lengths to which our hero was willing to go to help those he barely knew. Poor Owen, the brave Wormling, was spewed from the Kerrol along with pieces of the flyer, seawater, partially digested fish, seaweed, old wood, and stomach acid. Gallons of this unsavory mess projected the Wormling like a slingshot toward the shore.

"Aaaahhhhhhhhhh!" the boy yelled as he flew, finally landing with a splash about a hundred yards past the skiff.

"Paddle!" Mordecai shouted as the pointed horns at the top of the Kerrol's head disappeared into the murky water.

Owen awoke in the dark on the sandy shore, a hairy face hovering over him. "Mordecai," he whispered. A fire blazed in a pit nearby, people huddled around it, faces reflecting the orange glow. It was clear they had pulled apart the skiff to use for the fire.

"What happened down there?" Mordecai said.

Owen leaned up on his elbows. "There was no way to keep from falling into the Kerrol's mouth, so I just did everything I could to avoid those teeth. Remember that story from *The Book of the King* where the man is swallowed by the huge fish?"

Mordecai nodded. "At least you weren't in there three days."

"He wouldn't have been either if he'd had jargid skins in his shirt. I rubbed them on the Kerrol's stomach. He must be allergic."

Mordecai shook his head and pulled from his tunic a weathered manuscript. "Your notes on *The Book of the King*. You left this behind—why?"

"For you. So you might read and believe." Owen scanned the people by the fire. "Did everyone make it?"

Mordecai nodded.

"How will you get back?"

"I'm not going," Mordecai said. "Since you left I've regretted every moment I stayed. I should have come with you."

"Believe me, we could have used your help."

"I promised myself time and again that I would follow you, but each morning I looked at the tide and said, 'Not today, tomorrow.' But tomorrow never came. I stared at the sunset each night, remembering the times we shared, trying to imagine what you were going through. I know I let you down by staying. I'm sorry."

"What's done is done, friend," Owen said.

"I can't wait to hear of your adventures. Where is Watcher?"

Owen described what had happened at the Castle on the

Moor—how Watcher and their horse, Humphrey, had gone into hiding waiting for him.

"And what of *The Book of the King?*"

"Watcher has it as well as Mucker." Owen looked at the ground. "But the Dragon has my sword and the missing chapter."

"Missing chapter?"

Owen explained how he had heard of it from the Scribe, their fight with the vaxors, how he fooled the Dragon, his trip into the White Mountain to rescue the workers, and his eventual capture.

"You have been busy," Mordecai said. "When I saw the transport flyers taking their prisoners, I could stand it no longer. I set out against the tide, having no idea one would crash and that it would be you in the water."

"The King even used your indecision," Owen said. "As the book says, 'You were prepared for such a time as this.' It's not too late to go with us."

Mordecai studied him. "Any progress on finding the Son?"

"Oh, Mordecai—," Owen began.

The king of the west's armor bearer approached and bowed. He introduced himself as Dalphus. "The king would like an audience with you both when convenient."

Owen stood and brushed off his clothes. "We will come now. But first we have to douse this fire."

Dalphus stopped and turned. "The people need the warmth. Besides, you are not in charge here."

"Wisdom leads an army, Dalphus. And cunning. It is foolish to make a fire here. You'll alert every demon flyer and the Dragon himself of our whereabouts."

"Answer my question," Mordecai said, a hand on Owen's arm. "Have you found the Son?"

"You defy the rule of our sovereign?" Dalphus said. "He ordered this bonfire for the warmth of the people."

"If I know your sovereign, his wife ordered this fire." Owen kicked sand on the blaze as the people scattered. Mordecai joined in.

"We're cold!" the people cried.

"Who does he think he is?"

"Because he survived that sea monster he thinks he can do as he pleases."

Mordecai grabbed Owen's shoulder. "Tell me what you found, Wormling. Tell me about the Son. Does he live?"

Owen shook free and clenched his teeth. "He lives. And I will tell you but not now."

Owen's problem was that he himself wasn't completely convinced he was the Son. Every time the thought hit him that he had a father, a mother, a sister, and even a future bride, his heart leaped. But when he thought of the responsibility that came with Sonship, he backed away. How could he convince anyone to follow him if he didn't totally believe? He couldn't even get them to douse the fire without a fight.

The king and queen sat dry and warm beneath a lean-to. Even in this strange, rough setting, they bore the air of royalty. Owen bowed, but Mordecai approached them as if they were street people. Clearly more was going on here than polite conversation.

"Why did you put out the fire?" the queen said. "The king was bestowing warmth on his subjects."

"Your Highness," Owen said, "no rudeness was intended. But I know this country and what lurks in the shadows."

"You usurped the authority of your sovereign."

The king put a hand on her shoulder. "Dear, it's all right. I'm sure our friend is right. The fire could signal our enemies."

"Yes," Owen said, "and as soon as they discover a missing transport flyer, they'll come looking."

"Well, someone is going to have to take us from this place," the queen said. "We're in the middle of nowhere."

"I have friends a few miles that way," Owen said. "They shot the beast from the air."

"Some friends," the queen said. "They nearly got us killed. I should like to have a conversation with the leader of that team of archers."

"Young man," the king said, "tell us who you are. Back at the castle you pretended to be someone else."

"I am the Wormling," Owen said. "I came from the Highlands to find the Son of the King."

"How do we know he's not pretending now?" the queen said.

"Let him speak," Mordecai said.

Dalphus stepped close, but since he had no weapon and

Mordecai was almost twice his size (especially around the belly), he stepped back at the old man's glare.

"I know your daughter was taken from you when she was young," Owen said. "I know your heart breaks for her. I was given *The Book of the King*, which led me to your castle. I have been in search of the Son and . . ." Owen trailed off. His thoughts swirled. There was no explanation other than that he was the Son. He fit the prophecy. The wound on his heel. All the writings pointed to him.

The queen shifted. "Yes, go on. Go on."

Mordecai inched closer, and sweat trickled down Owen's neck. This was a thousand times worse than standing before a class and trying to speak, yet he was suddenly overcome with peace and a power he had never felt before. "I discovered the Son at the Castle on the Moor," he said.

The king rose. "In our castle? Who? What is his name?"

"You're lying," the queen said. "How could this person have been right under our noses?"

Owen cleared his throat and ran a foot through the sand. He whispered to the king, "The Son, the one who is to marry your daughter and unite the two worlds, the one who will lead a strong army against the Dragon and his forces . . ."

"Yes?" the king said.

"Yes?" the queen said.

"Yes?" Mordecai said.

Owen stepped back and spread his feet. "I am he."

There was a long silence as they merely stared. Owen heard only the water lapping at the shore.

And then came the laughter. Deep and hearty.

"You," the queen said, "the King's Son?" She doubled over, holding her stomach as she cackled.

The people gathered and laughed so hard they cried. The king looked away, smiling.

Mordecai simply studied Owen's face.

W ell, that couldn't have gone as well as you'd hoped," Mordecai said as he followed Owen from the laughter to the water's edge.

The moon reflected off the surface, and Owen wondered if demon flyers were near. He wished Watcher were with him.

"What about you?" Owen said finally. "Do you believe me? Or do you scoff too?"

"Of course I believe you," Mordecai said a little too quickly and without conviction. "I mean, I've always trusted you. Always believed . . ."

"You're among the first living souls who've heard this," Owen said. "You don't believe it at all."

Mordecai tossed seashells into the water. "I confess I pictured the Son a little taller, maybe a little older."

"See?" Owen said. "Even you don't believe."

"From what you have said about your travels, you have faced much danger with admirable courage. . . ." He moved closer and seemed to study Owen's head in the moon-light. "But there was no doubt injury, and I'm wondering whether—"

"Whether I hit my head and now I'm crazy? Believe me, I'd like nothing better than to have this all be a dream and wake up at home and just go to school tomorrow. I don't want to be the King's Son. I have not desired the responsibility or the station."

"But *The Book of the King* says, 'Great responsibility comes to those with a royal bloodline.' And perhaps the strange man who sought you out in the Highlands knew the truth."

"So you do believe me?"

Mordecai pressed his lips together. "I want to, lad, but how can you be both Wormling and Son?"

Owen sat in the sand, a chill wind whipping his face. "I struggle with that as well. But one does not negate the other. I am also from a small town in the Highlands and known as

Owen Reeder. That I was him does not make it impossible for me to be the Wormling, does it?"

Mordecai lowered himself heavily beside Owen. "It just seems strange that you were given a task that leads you to this discovery. It's almost as if you were deceived."

Owen shrugged. "But had I been told at the beginning that I was the King's Son, I would have run, frightened and unbelieving, daunted by the task ahead. Don't you see? It was all those days searching and training and hiking and learning that prepared me for the truth."

"But is it not also possible—" Mordecai paused, softening his voice, seeming to carefully choose his words—"that after all the searching and wrong turns, perhaps you talked yourself into believing that you were the one?"

"Why would I talk myself into something I would not have wished for in the first place? It was Nicodemus who helped me see."

"Nicodemus?"

"An angel. Invisible being. Whatever you want to call him. He showed me plainly what was directly in front of me."

Mordecai shrank back, his bearded face a question mark.

And so Owen began again, telling how each step of the way had led him to this conclusion. The wound on his foot that had become a scar. The words of the book.

Mordecai seemed to study him, his eyes finally softening.

Then came the sentence that warmed Owen's heart like nothing before. "And how will we get them to believe?"

"We? You believe? Truly?"

Mordecai struggled to his feet, and Owen joined him. "If what you say is true, it began long ago at your father's castle. Yes, I do believe. And I kneel before you now and . . ."

"Stand up, Mordecai. What is it?"

Clearly overcome with emotion, Mordecai said, "He has given me a second chance, just as you told me long ago. He knew I would run from my mistakes, that in my shame I would come here. He knew the jargid I loved so much would repel the Kerrol. He used even my mistakes to bring me back to himself."

"Who?" Owen said.

"Your father. The King. He has used even all this to show his great love for me." Mordecai threw his arms around Owen and wept.

Owen hugged him just as tightly, and when the man pulled away, he held Owen's shoulders firmly. "You are the Son of the King. I can see it in your eyes. Your life has been spared so that you can lead the army into battle, so that through your marriage, the two worlds will unite. I will follow wherever you lead, from this moment forward. I will again follow the King."

There on the cold beach under the soft moonlight, the army of the King received its first recruit.

✦✦✦

And as the laughter continued in the darkened camp, one small figure stood on a dune overlooking this scene, not laughing but looking on in wonder at the two whose voices carried over the water to his young ears.

The boy's heart welled within him as the two in the distance embraced, for he was the second recruit.

11

Gurgling

It has been our custom not to over-whelm you with too much gore, but we come now to an episode that must be shown in all its grotesquerie. If you are among the squeamish, you may want to skip to the next chapter. However, if you do, you may miss important information about the enemy's strategy.

The archenemy of our hero sat in his lair high above the Lowlands at the table with his council—including Slugspike, a hideous beast whose body was covered with scaly spines too sharp to touch. He had been called in by the Dragon as a last resort to discover the hiding place of the Wormling.

The Dragon picked at his teeth, perhaps trying to free some bit of fresh flesh of an underling who had not accomplished an assignment. He turned to his trusted aide, RHM, Reginald Handler Mephistopheles. His voice was raspy and grating as he studied a fingernail. "I said I wanted an answer to the Wormling's whereabouts. Is there no one who can bring me answers?"

"Sire, all available searchers are combing the countryside."

"All available?" the Dragon spat. "Which means some are not looking for him? Do you understand what is at stake? Why would you not send every searcher?"

"Some are in the Highlands guarding Onora, daughter of the king of the west, and Gwenolyn, daughter of the King."

"Keep one on Onora and pull the rest," the Dragon hissed. "I am through toying with this imp. I want his body. And the same for this Watcher of his. Kill them on sight—do not even attempt to bring them here for questioning."

"A wise decision, O great one," Slugspike said.

"And where is the Changeling?" the Dragon said. "If that truly was the Wormling in the Castle on the Moor pretending to be the Changeling, the real one must be somewhere in that swamp."

"Again, sire," RHM said, "we have all available—"

"I don't want to hear how many are available! I want to

hear that you have located even one of the enemies I seek! Do you not comprehend what is happening?"

The members of the council stared at the table. RHM bowed nearly to the floor as if hoping not to be consumed by the fire that gurgled in the Dragon's throat.

"We are close to realizing the magnificent dream I conceived so long ago," the Dragon said. "The King thrown down and crushed. All he has worked so hard to create snuffed out like his tiny life. And it all hinges on this Wormling, the only connection between the King and his Son." He leaned near to RHM. "We are so close, and yet, if this scamp escapes, there is still a chance he will succeed."

"You could always purify the land, O great one," Slugspike said.

"In due time. When my throne is stained with the blood of Onora and I have killed and buried the Son, then both worlds will worship me and I will cleanse the earth with fire."

The door flew open and in ran a small winged creature, talons pecking the floor. A deadly rattle surged in the Dragon's throat, causing the impudent intruder to slide to a stop and throw a wing over his face. "Begging your pardon for not knocking, Your Highness, but I bring news from Mirantha."

The Dragon turned toward an open window and let go the inferno along with a deafening roar. "That felt good," he muttered, a puff of black smoke escaping a nostril. "Once

I commit to fire, I can't hold it or it gives me indigestion. Now, what is it, messenger?"

"News from the waters of the Kerrol, sire. One of the transport flyers from the Castle on the Moor crashed into the water there. We spotted fire on the shore and found part of the cage."

"And what of the Kerrol?"

"He devoured the flyer, sire, but all the humans escaped."

"How could they possibly crash into the water and escape? Did anyone think to look for tracks in the sand?"

"The fire was hastily extinguished, but we found no footprints leading from the site."

The Dragon's eyes flashed. "You know what this means, RHM? The Wormling had to be in that group. He was with the transport! Who else would have been able to get out of that?"

"Would he have had arrows, Your Majesty?" the messenger said. "The Kerrol showed me more than a dozen that hit the flyer."

"He had help," the Dragon said. "He is beginning to marshal his forces. Now is the time to crush him. Sound the alarm. All who follow me must converge on this area." He retreated to a corner and pulled from a pile of rubble the gleaming Sword of the Wormling. "Send a message to the Lowlanders that anyone who brings me the body of the Wormling shall inherit his sword and an endless world of riches."

Slugspike rose. "Allow me, Your Greatness. I will find this defiler of your kingdom and bring his body back to you in pieces."

The Dragon smiled. "You want the riches."

"I want to wipe the earth of this brigand and to pave the way for your new kingdom." He bowed low, the spikes in his legs piercing the floor and emitting a slow leak of green that caused the others to draw back.

"Very well, Slugspike. Lead all my forces and find this Wormling. Kill him and bring what is left of him to me. I am safe as long as I have his sword. He can have the book. He can have his Watcher and whatever rabble he can surround himself with. This is the only thing that can kill me."

The Dragon sucked air through his teeth and dismissed all but RHM. "I have one more task for you," he said.

"Anything, sire."

He handed him a key ring. "Go to the Prisons of Shambal."

RHM's mouth fell open. "But, sire—"

"You said anything!"

"Yes, but—"

"You will bring me the minions of time. But keep your movements secret and the minions hidden."

Watcher awoke with a shiver as a chill wind blew through the cave. She searched the cave for any sign of the Wormling. It didn't require her special senses to know something was wrong. A whole night had passed since he should have joined her and Humphrey, and Watcher feared the worst.

I should have stayed with him. He told me to take the book and find shelter, but a good friend would have insisted on going with him.

She knew he would have argued until she gave up anyway. The Wormling was stubborn—almost as stubborn as she. She smiled at that despite her dread.

Watcher's entire life had centered on waiting for the Wormling. She had faithfully done her job until he finally emerged from the other world. Then she had joined him on his adventure to find the Son, leaving her quiet life above the Valley of Shoam and all she had known. But what now? What if the Wormling did not return?

If Watcher was not careful, she could fill every waking moment with such fear. Her dreams were already crowded with Dragons and flames and trying to protect the Wormling.

Each time doubt and indecision crept up on her, she tried to recall passages from *The Book of the King*, like this one:

> Search diligently for the King's realm and his goodness, and you will be given everything you need. Don't worry about what will happen tomorrow. Tomorrow will take care of itself.

Easier said than done. Did this apply to her, an animal (though a smart one) in a world of human words and wisdom? Did the King have a plan for her life as well?

Watcher tried to still her troubled heart with thoughts of how far she and the Wormling had come. He had grown strong, and it felt as if they were being drawn toward something—like the tide draws small sea creatures and shells to the shore.

Humphrey, standing there sleeping and snoring as horses

do, snorted and fluttered his lips—sometimes frightening Watcher in the night. He looked like a statue except for the occasional twitch or ripple of his great flank muscles. He was strong and steady and clearly smarter than he appeared. If only she could understand horse language. She missed conversations. The Wormling always seemed to calm her heart.

A strip of light invaded the cave as the clouds turned orange and pink. Watcher's ears twitched with excitement. She loved this time of day, when everything seemed new and fresh. Hearing something, she slipped outside to a path leading to the rocks above the entrance, where she had left a ripped piece of material. She and the Wormling had agreed this would signal her location. It flapped in the breeze.

A querrlis hopped among the branches of a tree, its long, bushy tail twitching, black eyes scanning the ground. Watcher knew it was searching for food. Winter was coming.

The animal barked and showed her its sharp front teeth, then munched a nut and buried itself in a hole in the tree.

Watcher moved back inside the cave. "I feel it too, little one." The sky felt full of invisibles, all heading in the same direction. She had never felt such strength and power and evil.

They're searching for the Wormling.

Humphrey stepped up behind her and nudged her with his snout.

"Something bad is happening," Watcher whispered. "And if they're looking for him, they're also looking for us."

Mucker, the worm the Wormling had used to get from the Highlands to the Lowlands, stirred in Watcher's fur. She couldn't help but fear for him as well.

Owen could not convince the king and queen of the west that they needed to move from the shore. He nearly left without them when they again laughed at him and his notion of being the King's Son. It wasn't until Mordecai thundered, "You'll become stew for the Kerrol!" that they picked up their things and followed.

A storm was brewing. The people walked side by side in small groups, Owen leading them and Mordecai bringing up the rear. At times they were forced to walk single file because stone walls rose on either side.

The queen appeared aghast that she

had to walk. It bothered Owen that these were the parents of the girl he would one day marry—if he had understood the prophecy correctly. Would his wife be like her mother, demanding to be carried about? Would she whine and moan about rocky crevasses? If she looked like her mother, she would be beautiful, but even that would not make up for attitude.

"I must rest!" the queen cried out. "I am fatigued."

"Choose fatigue or death," Mordecai called from behind.

"I simply can't go another step," the woman said.

"We'll leave you, then," Mordecai said. "Better one die rather than the whole company."

"Why must you scare us?" the queen sobbed. "You're worse than the Dragon."

"Madam," Mordecai said, "if you think that, you have not met the Dragon."

"But I have," she whimpered. "With him, you can negotiate, bargain. With you, there is no compromise."

"You really think you can reason with the Dragon? There is no negotiating with—"

"That's not true," she said. "We negotiated a treaty with him concerning our daughter."

"And what did the Dragon say just before he threw you in that cage?" Owen said, nostrils flaring. "He said your daughter's blood would anoint his throne. So much for your treaty."

"He felt betrayed," she spat, glaring at her husband. "If you hadn't helped this urchin, we wouldn't be here now."

"He saved our lives from that sea beast," the king said.

"Oh, I forgot," she said. "My mistake. Our future son-in-law. A commoner!"

"Enough," Mordecai said, dragging two logs from a clearing. The king and two other men helped the queen onto the logs as Mordecai and Owen struggled under the weight.

"Comfy now?" Mordecai said.

"The bark is a little rough," she said.

The sky grew darker, and Owen thought he heard strange sounds over the footsteps trudging around him. The castle dwellers seemed unaccustomed to traveling, but Owen was grateful to be on the ground and not in the water or the air.

"Small creatures up in the rocks," a young boy said, pointing.

"Good," Owen said. "They're friends. The reason we escaped the transport flyer."

"The ones who shot at us?" the queen said.

"Halt!" someone said from above.

"Erol!" Owen called. "It's me! I've brought friends from the Castle on the Moor."

"I wouldn't call them that," Mordecai muttered.

Erol stared down, smiling. "I never thought you'd be back."

"Help us up. There's a strange storm brewing, and—"

"That's more than a storm," Erol said. "There are also invisibles and demon flyers about."

14

The Storm

The children of Erol led Owen and the others in a prancing procession to the main cavern. Starbuck, Erol's son, and many of the others Owen had helped rescue from the Badlands were there, whooping and singing as they danced along. Like a howling wind the storm descended, and Owen was glad to have everyone inside.

Erol welcomed Owen with a hug, and the company sang to him. The people of the castle huddled in the back, apparently afraid of these creatures, but Owen felt as if he had returned home.

"Tell us of your travels," Erol said.

"In time," Owen said. "But I have to know. I heard from villagers that you met with foul play by the Dragon, that he had blasted you and your clan from the mountain."

"We're doing the attacking," Starbuck said, beaming.

"That's right," Erol said. "We shot down a transport flyer just yesterday."

"We know," Owen said. "We were the ones in the cage."

Erol's mouth dropped. "You? And all of these? How did you survive?"

After Owen told the story, Erol shook his head and said, "Well, other than the Dragon's attempt to steal our children, which you foiled, we have not been attacked. Though we have felt an uneasy presence at times." He leaned close. "Interlopers sent by you know who."

Owen nodded, then introduced the king and queen of the west.

Erol bowed low. "Forgive the mess, Your Highnesses."

Erol's wife, Kimshi, blushed. "If I'd known we had royalty coming, I would have put my husband to work cleaning."

The king spoke. "Your dwelling is fine. Thank you for the hospitality. Especially the music. It's been so long since I've heard such wonderful sounds."

The queen ran a finger along a dusty table and sneered.

"Play something else," a young man from the castle said. "Something fit for a king and queen."

The musicians gathered in the main room, and Erol counted time with his foot and bow. The bright and airy music made the clan of Erol dance. Owen couldn't help but clap and stomp along.

The music suddenly stopped when a hulking figure entered, stooping low. His face was grimy, and his shoulders slumped from carrying the queen. Owen wondered why it had taken Mordecai so long to come inside—did he fear these friends, or was he simply unaccustomed to such crowds?

"It's him," Erol said nervously, gathering his children and wife.

"This is my friend," Owen said. "His name is Mor—"

"I know his name. He cursed us many years ago as he went through here on his way to the island. Back to torment us?"

Mordecai spoke softly. "I was angry and hurt and wanted to die. But the King's hand was with me despite it all. He sent the Wormling to me. He came to learn, but he taught much more. And if he calls you his friend, you are friends of mine as well. Can you forgive an old man?"

Erol studied him warily, his face finally lightening. "We can, but not without food and more song. Kimshi, prepare a feast. We shall dine on the meat of forgiveness."

A clap of thunder racked the mountainside and echoed off

the walls. Children dived under tables, and the castle dwellers huddled.

"Do your caverns flood?" the king said.

Erol gazed at the ceiling and shivered. "That's not a rainstorm, Your Highness. That's a storm of a different sort. Something terrible is being unleashed in the invisible kingdom."

Runners came from above, filling the narrow passages. "Demon flyers, sir. Along with every death machine of the Dragon. They're sounding the mountain. We had to abandon our posts."

"Everyone take shelter in the depths," Erol said. "Starbuck, lead our guests."

"What is sounding?" Owen said.

Erol grabbed him by the arm and hurried along the passage. "They send waves that search for warm bodies. Deep inside these walls we won't be detected, but we must hurry."

15

A New Song

As the storm raged and the soundings continued, Owen, Erol, and Mordecai met in a secluded spot. Though Owen had revealed his identity to the king and queen, he still felt uneasy about talking with the castle dwellers about himself. But he had no reservations in speaking openly with Erol.

The being's eyes glistened in the firelight. When Owen explained what he had learned about himself, Erol dropped to his knees and bowed his head.

"I have no reason to doubt you," he whispered. "I can tell by the fire that burns within you that you are the true Son of the King."

Erol immediately summoned his people and told them the news.

Gasps filled the cavern as young and old, men and women covered their mouths, fell to their knees, or moved closer for a better look.

Starbuck leaned against a wall, half hidden in the dim light.

"I'm no different than I was before, Starbuck," Owen said.

"No different? This changes everything. As the Wormling, you lived among us, talked with us, even came to our rescue. But now . . ."

Erol leaned close. "We have taught him that royalty is separate. They live in castles and eat food prepared by hired hands. Like them." He nodded to the king and queen of the west. "They keep to themselves. They do not associate with our kind because we are lowly and different."

Dalphus stood in front of the king and queen to protect them.

"That's not as it should be," Owen said. "And that's not the way it will be in the King's household."

"In your father's household," Mordecai said.

Owen shuddered. "I don't know the King, don't remember him from my infancy. But I know in my heart that he would be pleased to call you his friend, Starbuck. And you, Erol. And you. All of you. There is no difference between people of low estate and high. We all come from the same dust."

Mordecai scratched his beard. "Doesn't *The Book of the King* say something about our being equal in the King's sight?"

Owen nodded and recited:

> "Those who put their hope in the King will never be disappointed. It doesn't matter if you are rich or poor, if you dwell in fertile lands or the desert, if you are praised among men or an outcast. There is one King, and he is generous and kind to anyone who asks for his help. All who call on him receive his love."

Starbuck looked on, eyes wide. "How do you remember all that?"

Owen touched his chest. "The words were not written simply on the page. They were written on my heart. And each day they grow deeper and become part of me."

"What would you have us do?" Erol said. "Anything you ask . . ."

"Do not be so quick in your promises," Mordecai said. "You have no idea what he might ask."

"And do not be so quick in your judgments," Erol said. "We may seem a gentle breed of singers, but our hearts are fiercely loyal to the King and his descendants."

"A great battle lies ahead," Owen said. "I'm only now beginning to realize what that means. Before, I simply thought it would be the Son's responsibility. Now I understand I am the Son."

"What can we do?" Erol said.

"Sing a new song—and not just here but throughout the land."

"Singing is still forbidden; is it not?" Mordecai said.

"By edict of the evil one," Erol said. "I have no problem defying him."

"Many will hear your song and believe. They will follow you. Use all the instruments at your disposal, all the skill of the singers, all the harmonies that please the ear."

"What shall be our theme?"

"That a new day is coming. After the fight is over and the battle is won, the King will establish his kingdom in every heart and unite every person from the Highlands and the Lowlands. There shall be no more division of clans, no more war, no more fighting with the Dragon, for he shall be defeated."

"Cast out?" Erol said.

"Utterly."

"We won't have to hide any longer, won't have to keep our songs to ourselves."

"But what I'm asking you to do now is perhaps more dangerous than the battle itself. You'll be exposed to the enemy as you sing."

Erol's eyes were wet. "We will not be able to take part in the battle?"

Owen pulled Erol close. "You will be by my side. I want to hear your victory song after the Dragon falls."

"Then we have work to do," Erol said, rising. "Bring the instruments and a parchment. We will sing a new song!"

16

The Nestor

RHM returned from the Prisons of Shambal under cover of night. He bore two black cases, one large and clearly harder to carry than the other because of something struggling to get out.

RHM remained discreet, flying along the tops of the trees in the darkened forests. He rehearsed what he would say to his liege, every nuance, every syllable. One wrong move, even a perceived mistake, could mean his life.

When he drew close to the clearing below the Dragon's castle, he shot straight into the sky and ascended to the lair. Sentries came brandishing fire wands until they recognized him and waved him onward. RHM could tell they were intrigued by the cases, but they knew better than to inquire.

RHM flew directly to the parapet at the highest point of the castle, where his master would be. Flapping his wings noisily to warn the Dragon, he stepped onto the stones and set the black cases down a moment, keeping them ever in his sight.

The Dragon huddled in a corner, devouring some grotesque meaty flesh, slopping and crunching.

"Sire, I have brought what you requested," RHM said, bowing low.

The Dragon turned, teeth red with the blood of another victim. He wiped his lips and approached the cases gingerly, studying them. "Any trouble with the pod?"

"They haven't hatched, so the timing seems almost perfect. A good call on your part, sire."

"Yes," the Dragon growled. "And is the nestor in that case?" He peeked inside but stayed a good distance away. "It looks rather large." Moving closer, he scraped a razor-sharp talon along the top of the case like fingernails on a chalkboard.

RHM nodded. "The nestor has not enjoyed being cooped up away from its little ones."

The Dragon's eyes gleamed in the fading moonlight as he

cocked his head and put an ear to the side of the case as if listening for the heartbeat of an unborn child. "There, there," he cooed. "You'll be out and on your way soon."

The case shook violently, and the Dragon recoiled. "It wants out," he said. "Open it."

"But, sire, there is a good chance—"

"Open it," the Dragon snarled. "You can see that even my voice soothes it."

RHM weighed his response. He could play it safe and simply do as the Dragon suggested. However, if the nestor escaped, the Dragon would blame him, and he would be incinerated on the spot.

"Your Highness, your wish is my command. But I fear—" RHM saw his master's eyes narrow. "Very well, sire."

RHM loosed the leather bindings from both sides, then unwound the cord from a circular block. Lastly, he used a small key to unfasten the locks, all the while holding down the lid.

"Come to me, beautiful nestor," the Dragon purred, like a child coaxing a puppy from a travel container.

RHM released the lid, and a hideous creature flopped forward on thin wings. Its body seemed too large for its spiny legs, and when it looked up at the Dragon with multiple eyes, it seemed to fawn before him, relaxing and rolling its wings underneath its body.

"There, there," the Dragon said. "You see? Gentle and cuddly like a baby."

Suddenly the creature puffed like an adder, and its wings shot out. With a burst and an intense buzz, it sped into the air.

RHM fell back, shrieking, but the Dragon stood straight, watching.

The nestor dived for the Dragon's back, opening its mouth and plunging down. It banged off a hard-as-rock scale and hung suspended a moment. Before the creature could dart away, the Dragon swatted it against a wall. It crunched there, slid to the floor, and lay still.

RHM moved carefully behind the Dragon. "Is it . . . dead?"

"With any luck, it's only stunned. Get it back in the case."

RHM cautiously stepped toward the body, pausing at the hideous face and daggerlike teeth that sent a shiver through him. He threw the box over it, carefully brought the lid up, and locked it.

Immediately the box buzzed and shook.

"And you say the hive is nearly fully developed?" the Dragon said.

"Yes, sire. The keeper said the ripening is nearly complete. Each tiny spot is an individual minion and below that another and another until you reach the center. The limited kronos venom is released through the teeth. Each sting releases a single drop into the bloodstream of the human target. Any more than that and the victim would shrivel and die within a day or two."

The Dragon skulked back to the corner and bit another piece of meat and began to chew. The large case continued to rattle and buzz as the Dragon slurped red liquid from a goblet and belched.

"Prepare for one more journey," the Dragon said. He explained the precise direction and how to break through the invisible barrier to the Highlands.

"You will see from the air a burned-out and charred house. Take the nestor into the cellar and hang the pod on a rafter. Leave the cord tied around the nestor's case. It will eventually chew through it."

"And it will stay with the pod?"

"Other than gathering food, yes. The pod is its life. Until the minions mature, the nestor will nurture them."

"How long before they break free and accomplish your task?"

The Dragon licked his lips, and his eyes shimmered. "Long before the humans in the Highlands recognize their need for me. They will beg. They will weep. The pain of quick years under the minions' sting will bring them low. And they will honor me as their sovereign.

"It won't be long now. Whether the Wormling lives or

dies, whether the Son shows himself or not, the two worlds will unite under my supremacy. The Highlanders, who know nothing of me, who don't even believe our realm exists, will learn of me and feel my wrath. And they will bow and call me king."

17

Rogers

Owen stayed underground with
the people of the castle and the
musicians of Erol for two days, avoid-
ing the searching eyes of the invisibles
who screeched and flew above. The
king and queen of the west had
retreated to a sectioned-off portion
of the cave with their servants, still
clearly wary of Owen and the musicians. Erol's clan had food to last a
whole winter season, and the meals—
and music—were excellent.

However, Owen grew restless,
wishing he could communicate with
Watcher and wanting to continue
his journey as quickly as possible. He
consulted with Mordecai and Erol and

also included Starbuck, knowing that he needed fresh, young minds in significant decisions, for he himself had been quite young when his mission had begun.

"You have no sword," Mordecai said.

"Erol will lend me a weapon."

"One that heals?" Mordecai said.

"I have nothing like that," Erol said. "But our swords and arrows are newly sharpened."

"Why not raise an army from throughout the land?" Mordecai said. "Prepare for battle? It would be much safer."

"Followers of the King are not called to safety," Owen said.

"You are more than a follower. You are the Son."

"There are things you do not know, Mordecai."

"Then tell me."

"You must trust me."

Mordecai ran a hand through his hair, his bulbous nose shining in the firelight. "No explanation needed. I would follow you into the Dragon's lair itself if you asked. But for the sake of the people, especially those who do not know you . . ."

Starbuck offered to recruit warriors as well, and then a deep voice resonated off the walls. "I'll go too."

Owen turned, surprised. "What are you doing there in the shadows?"

"Just listening, sir," a boy said, stepping into the light to reveal scruffy hair and beady eyes, not to mention a frame much too tiny for the sonorous voice. "I couldn't help overhearing."

"He's a spy for the king of the west," Mordecai said.

Owen smiled and beckoned the lad. "What's your name?"

"Rogers, sir."

"Are your parents here?"

"No, sir. I'm a stable boy for the king. He was kind enough to take me in when my parents were killed."

"Killed how?" Mordecai said, leaning forward, inspecting the boy.

"A fire, sir. I was gathering water when it happened."

"Any idea how it started?" Owen said.

"An attack. I heard wings flapping as I returned, and then I found our cabin engulfed in flames."

"Sounds familiar, Mordecai, doesn't it?" Owen said. Mordecai himself had been taken in by the true King when just a boy. Eventually the King made him captain of the guard to protect the King's family. His failure to protect the King's children sent him into a self-imposed exile.

Mordecai stared at the boy. "How did you get over here without our knowing?"

Rogers shrugged. "It is my gift. I am able to walk ever so lightly, even on dry ground. I saw you both at the beach the other night and heard everything you said. I vowed I would follow you into battle."

Owen patted the boy on the head. "We can use a disappearing artist like you. Train yourself to be even quieter and stay close to me. You will be part of the battle."

Starbuck squinted in the darkness. "You'll need more than waifs. You need strong warriors. Thousands of them."

"It is not the size of the army that wins the battle," Owen said. "We should not trust in our own power or strength. Indeed, *The Book of the King* says, 'Some trust in archers, others in their swords, but the one who trusts in the King shall have victory.' My goal is to follow him every step of the way and trust his leading. He has not failed me yet."

"You can't even remember your father," Mordecai said.

"But I have felt him here all my life." Owen touched his chest. "Even when I did not know that the man who called himself my father in the Highlands was simply playing a trick on me."

"Sir?" Rogers said. "Does the book explain why the King went away? why the people have lived in such fear for so long?"

Owen nodded. "Not in so many words, but it does talk about our enemy and how he plots. The first thing he did here after the King left was to outlaw singing. He takes the joy from life and replaces it with duty and rules. He kills and destroys to instill fear and compel you to follow, rather than ask you to follow.

"You see, the King, my father, gives life. He is like a bubbling spring, gushing to overflowing, bidding everyone to come and drink. When we do, we take our place in his grand design."

"Which is what?" Rogers said.

"Wholeness. Unity." Owen interlaced his fingers. "A union so deep inside that it defies explanation. We can't even conceive it yet. For us and those in the Highlands."

"It sounds wonderful."

"It's what the King had in mind all along until the Dragon rebelled. And that sent a ripple tearing through both worlds—and the invisible one above them."

Owen stood as the queen approached with several ladies of her court. He blushed and stared at the floor when they looked at him, and his mouth felt full of cotton. *How am I ever going to marry someone if I can't even look women in the face?*

"I come with a proposal," the queen announced as if everyone should heed what she said. "We were caged by the Dragon and then escaped. If we return and call for a meeting, he will see we are not rebels and that we act in good faith."

"To what end?" Owen said.

"A treaty, of course."

Mordecai sighed and shook his head. "You want to hand

the Son over to the Dragon in return for your daughter. I wouldn't trade this young man for a hundred daughters."

Owen put a hand on Mordecai's shoulder. "Careful—that's my bride you're talking about."

Mordecai's face fell. "I meant no offense to you."

Owen turned back to the queen. "And what does your husband say about this proposal?"

"The king is . . . not well. I am speaking for him."

"You speak treason against the true King," Mordecai said.

Like Watcher had read the skies and as Owen himself had pored over books, he now read between the lines of the woman's life. He stepped close and whispered, "You have not always lived in the Lowlands, have you?"

She stepped back, ashen. "Why would you say such a thing?"

"My father's book describes what happened when his children were taken, how it broke his heart. But it also describes the bride as coming from the Highlands. She was not taken, was she? It was you and your husband who were brought here."

She waved and glanced at the servants, plainly speechless.

"Tell the truth," Owen said. "In your world, an agreement is binding on both parties. That is your way and the way of your people."

"You're not really a queen?" someone said.

"And the king is not really a king?" another said.

"I must go," the queen said.

"No!" Owen said. "I know you care about your daughter and want her back. I want what is best for her and for you and your husband. It is my job to mend what is broken. To heal what is sick. To restore that which has been torn apart. And an agreement with the evil one will not accomplish that."

The woman inched closer, gathering her dress. "If you are the Son—and I am not saying you are—surely you would know that your own father made a treaty. The Dragon told us the King so despaired over the loss of his children that he promised the entire kingdom to the Dragon if he would spare them."

"Lies!" Mordecai shouted, spitting. "My King would never have promised such a thing."

"It's not her you don't believe," Owen said. "The Dragon is the liar and has been from the beginning. Lying is his language. It is true the King made a treaty and swore to keep it. But truth of that agreement will be revealed only at the right time."

"So you admit to this," the queen said.

"I admit that my father loves me—and all of you—enough to protect us from the consequences of the treaty. When it is revealed, we will understand. Now, though it feels at times like we're moving through a darkened corridor, we must trust that he is good and that in the end he will make things plain."

"You are a blind follower," the queen said, sneering. "You're no royal Son."

"And you are no queen," Mordecai muttered. "I only hope your daughter does not take after you."

Watcher darted out occasionally
for food for her and Humphrey,
but she mostly spent time inside the
cave brooding. The demon flyers and
other invisibles were plentiful—it
made her shake that they were so
numerous and this time made strange
noises. But the longer they stayed in
the air, the better. She hoped that
meant the Wormling had not been
located.

When the noise subsided and she
finally ventured out, she asked Humphrey to stay behind, for he was much
too large and lumbering to hide. She
began with short walks that gradually
became longer the more comfortable

she became with her surroundings. Numerous caves with dark entrances abounded, and the soft marsh was nearby with singing crickets and frogs. It wasn't the mountain she had grown up on, but it wasn't a bad place to wait for her friend.

One afternoon as she walked farther than ever, she heard a deep bang of rock against rock echoing through the trees.

Watcher hurried toward it. "Hello?" she called.

The banging continued until she heard a huge rockslide inside one of the caves. The banging stopped, and the frogs and crickets ceased their chatter.

Watcher rushed across a soft area, hooves splashing, and came upon a cave opening with dust billowing forth.

Someone coughed and sputtered, as if trying to catch his breath.

"Are you all right?" she said. "Hello?"

A human cough. Familiar.

She peered into the murky opening. "Need help in there?"

"Yes!" Rocks moved. Footsteps approached her.

Watcher gasped as a young man wiped dirt from his eyes and shook a cloud of dust from his hair. "I don't believe it," she said.

He wheezed and said, "What's the matter? Never seen a Wormling before?"

19

Planting

RHM followed the instructions of the Dragon to the letter and found himself in the Highlands. It was early morning before the sun was up, something for which RHM was grateful. He had never been to the wretched Highlands with all its houses and cars and traffic and lights and noise, noise, noise.

A thin strip of orange lit the clouds as he perched on a rooftop and faced east. The first rays of the sun peeked over the nearby mountain, and people began to stir. He wondered what they would do if any happened to spot him. He assumed they would scream and call the police—but he was much too fast, much too smart, much too agile to be caught.

Something startled him from behind, and he turned quickly. It was Mugrim, one of the Dragon's sentries. He was among the master's most trusted but not at all liked by the others in the court, least of all RHM.

"Ah, Reginald," Mugrim said. "So nice of you to . . . drop in."

"I haven't come for you, if that's what you're wondering."

"Here for an update on the bride-to-be?" Mugrim said.

"Is that what you're doing? Watching the bride?"

"Indeed."

"Then why were you slumbering behind that chimney? You wouldn't want me to relate that to the boss, would you?"

Mugrim smirked. "I've been watching this house for some time. Until the lights come on, there's no reason to get excited."

A light flickered in the main room.

"Then I suppose this is your big moment, Mugrim. Good luck."

"Wait, wait, Reginald. What do you have there?"

"None of your business."

"Mmm. Buzzing. Anything important?"

RHM cursed and grabbed the cases. "Just get back to your job." He flew away, just above housetops.

A man heading to his car in the dim light looked up and
did a double take. "What in the world?"

RHM kept moving, flying higher, trying to remember the
landmarks the Dragon had mentioned. He saw the knoll in
the distance where the Dragon had put an end to Mr. Page, as
he had called himself. There was the movie theater. And the
restaurant where the girl Clara worked. Of course, that was
not her real name.

In an area near homes and businesses that seemed worse
than shabby, RHM found the remnants of the house the
Dragon had described. It looked as if it had been beautiful
once long ago. He descended through the top and flew down
a staircase to the water-filled basement. A foul stench reached
RHM as he tiptoed quickly to the end of the room.

He hated standing water. Liquid turned his talons to mush,
and he couldn't attack a thing. He sloshed along, the cases
under his wings. At the far end of the room, he found the
opening with a shaft below. He opened the small case and
pulled out the huge hive, bell-shaped and light, as if filled
with air. But it was filled with much more than that.

He hung it on the cable, made sure it was secure, and went
to work on the larger case. He loosened the leather straps so
the nestor could work itself free. Then he opened the latches
with the tiny key and stood back.

The buzzing stopped. A hideous hiss came from inside the case, and something sliced through one of the leather bands.

"Dear me," RHM said, backing away in the water, heart beating wildly.

Another band snapped, and a buzz-hiss-gurgle came from the case.

RHM gasped in terror and flew toward the opening above, rocketing skyward, unwilling to even look back.

20

Ghost Town

As if pulled by an unseen force, pushed onward by what he knew he had to do, Owen traveled to the Valley of Zior. It was just as he remembered it, a sweltering place of death. Other areas of the Lowlands had turned cold under a blanket of snow, but the desert remained as foreboding as ever. Mordecai seemed to stare in disbelief at the bony carcasses of demon flyers.

"The Wormling did that," Starbuck said.

"How?" Rogers said, gazing at Owen as if he were a superstar.

"The Sword of the Wormling is a splendid weapon," Owen said.

"Which you do not have with you," Mordecai said.

"You seem to enjoy reminding me of that. But we have the weapons from Erol."

"Sticks and sharpened rocks," Mordecai said. "If what you tell me about these skittering lizards is true, we'll need a lot more than these."

They traveled through the desert during the day, which they could never have done in the summer, and through part of a night. Owen couldn't help remembering how Watcher had reacted to this place. He wondered how she and Humphrey were doing.

Owen searched the darkness for the eyes of lizard scouts but noticed only the outline of the cave ahead.

"It's too quiet," Starbuck said, whirling to look behind them. "Maybe they're planning an ambush."

"Who?" Rogers said.

"The lizards. Or the Dragon's workers. Or both." Starbuck shivered and slowed.

"Don't worry," Owen said. "I won't let them take you down into that mountain again."

Owen noticed small lumps here and there across the rolling sand. He uncovered one with his foot and revealed a lizard skeleton. It struck him that they were walking on the backs of lizards all the way to the encampment.

"What could have killed them?" Starbuck said.

"I'm just glad they're dead," Mordecai said.

The camp had clearly not been touched in months. Sand covered the fire pits. Chains and leg-irons were half buried. Shells of buildings looked out onto empty streets and wooden sidewalks.

A helmet and breastplate lay by a torn tent, a piece of the animal's skin flapping in the breeze. Owen recalled that the powerful and cruel creature had been a sentry that looked part ape, part rhinoceros. The being's horn had protruded above its helmet.

"The people were here," Owen whispered. "Men and women and children huddling for warmth, all chained."

"The holding pens were right there," Starbuck said. "We slept here each night before they took us into the cave."

Owen moved up the narrow path to the mouth of the cave. No guards, no noise, no light.

"You say the true Queen was held here?" Mordecai asked.

"That way," Owen said. "Stay here and keep watch. I'll check inside."

Owen moved into pitch-darkness and stopped to let his eyes adjust. He might as well have kept them closed. He felt his way along with a hand on the wall and came to a small indentation on the left where he had climbed and stayed until he could get to the Queen.

He crossed the passage and felt his way through the door, bumping into a chair. This was where he had met the Queen.

"It's been years since I let myself believe he was even still alive," the Queen had said about her Son. About Owen. *"Find my Son. Tell him where I am. Forget the unity of the worlds, the talk of peace and love and tranquility. Just bring my Son to me."*

Owen pushed the chair until it hit the table. When he reached to support himself, he touched something hairy on the tabletop. It moved and he recoiled, nearly falling.

"Who's there?" a man's raspy voice said.

The table creaked and Owen sensed someone moving toward him. Smelled him, that is. A terrible odor. Sour breath. The stench triggered a memory—like familiar words from a page read long ago. Fingers found Owen's face. Then a cackling laugh.

"You're not one of the guards. Skin's too soft."

"I am the Wormling," Owen managed. "Who are you?"

"The Wormling!" the man gasped. "You kept your promise! You returned!" He grabbed Owen with both hands, then let go and wept.

"What's wrong, old man? Where have they taken the Queen and the others?"

"It's been many days. A new shipment of workers was to come in cages by transport flyers. But one of them didn't show, and everyone was taken away."

"Except you."

"I hid in a crevice below. I would not have survived the journey anyway."

Owen pulled the man up and aided him to the cave entrance, where Mordecai gave him a drink from their water skin. The man was so pale after working underground that he looked like a ghost.

"What did you do here?" Mordecai said.

"What we were told," he said. "Dug precious metals and collected them. The transport flyers carried them to the Dragon. I overheard a guard talking one night about the Dragon using gems and some kind of liquid that would purify the kingdom."

"What liquid would do that?" Starbuck said.

"In the White Mountain," Owen said. "It bubbles up, and mixed with fire, it explodes. He has the source for the fire, he has the liquid, but he won't be satisfied with a small explosion. The gems will create fiery missiles that will blast throughout the land." He turned back to the old man. "Where did they take the Queen and the other prisoners?"

He shrugged. "The only other place they've ever mined is Diamondhead, which is even more remote than this. Legend says they must use transport flyers just to bring in the sun. If that's where they took them, old and young will die from the cold. And I fear the Queen will as well."

"The Dragon must be ramping up the production of gemstones so he can destroy us all," Owen said.

"Why would he destroy the earth?" Starbuck said.

Mordecai gritted his teeth. "He would do anything to defy the King. And if he can destroy the beauty the King has made and fashion it in his own ugly likeness, he will."

"But why would the King allow this?" Rogers said.

"He won't," Owen said. "The Dragon will fail. That's why he sent us."

"Us?" Starbuck said. "Surely you don't mean that the four of us—"

"Have faith, young man," Owen said. "The King's purposes will not fail because of numbers." He faced Mordecai. "Take these three with you and return to Erol. Tell him to send the whole clan throughout the land, bidding others to join the fight. Sing songs of deliverance. Tell people they have seen the Son and that he will soon return to lead them to battle."

"And what will you do?" Mordecai said. "Charge into that mine alone to rescue the prisoners?"

Owen clapped Mordecai on the shoulder. "I do not go alone. My father walks with me. And I do his bidding. And when I return, I will have more recruits."

"How can that be?" Starbuck said.

"Because every captive set free becomes a loving servant of the King."

Mordecai reached for the man, but he pulled away. "I may be old, but you don't have to carry me like a baby. That water invigorated these bones. Let's go."

"Meet me at the White Mountain," Owen said. "I'll be there with anyone who wants to follow."

"Why there?" Mordecai said.

Owen smiled. "You'll see, my friend."

Watcher had squealed so loudly at the Wormling's return that Humphrey galloped out and found them laughing and talking. The Wormling said he had escaped the clutches of the Dragon but had gotten sidetracked by a demon flyer. While hiding he had fallen into a dark tunnel, become trapped in a rockslide, and had to dig his way out. Thus, all the dirt.

"You were fortunate you weren't killed," Watcher said.

Humphrey harrumphed and pawed at the ground.

"I'm ravenous," the Wormling said. "Is there anything to eat?"

Watcher walked him back to the cave and brought him fruit. "Where do we go from here?" she said.

"We still must find the Son, but we don't have *The Book of the King* or my sword—"

"I have the book," Watcher said, retrieving it for him. "Remember? You gave it to me for safekeeping."

The Wormling cradled the book and sighed. "Oh, Watcher, you're so faithful. When I am made a prince or a landowner or whatever the Son bestows upon me, I shall give you houses and lands and wonderful jewelry."

Watcher's smile faded. "You're planning to stay?"

Humphrey harrumphed again.

"I'm keeping my options open," the Wormling said. "Things change so fast. Let's talk of our next task."

"I do not want you to go away alone again," Watcher said. "Please promise we won't have to separate."

"I promise. Wherever I go, you will go." He patted Humphrey on the flank, and the horse stepped back and blew air through his lips. "All three of us will go. We will never be separated again. And we will kill that pesky Dragon and throw him down! That's exactly what we're going to do."

Watcher's eyes brimmed with tears. But just as quickly, the hair on her back stood up. "Something is out there. A demon flyer or . . . worse."

The Wormling stood. "Stay here. I'll check it out."

Watcher stayed in the shadows as the Wormling crept out. It seemed like an eternity.

Humphrey nickered, clearly trying to tell her something.

"Oh, friend," she whispered, "I wish I could understand you."

The horse threw his head back, strutted, even swished his tail.

Watcher could only shake her head.

From outside the cave came the sounds of a fierce fight and the Wormling calling for her. Watcher ran out to find him holding a stick before a demon sentry, its wings in battle position.

"Stay back, Watcher!" the Wormling yelled. "I'll kill this beast."

"With a stick?"

The Wormling turned back to the enemy and wielded the crude weapon. "Now you die! For the King and his Son and for all that is good!" He flung the stick at the sentry, hitting him in the chest, and he fell.

Watcher ran to the Wormling, who was panting as he knelt.

"Do not think me brave. I simply did what I had to do. The Wormling must protect his friends and find the Son. Now let's go."

Watcher moved to examine the dead beast, but the Wormling called out, "Careful! Don't go near it! Anyway, we must go right away."

She turned toward the cave.

"Right now, Watcher!" he shouted.

"You don't want me to leave *The Book of the King*, do you?"

The Wormling laughed. "Silly me. Of course not. Run and fetch it."

From inside she heard the Wormling scolding Humphrey. When she emerged, the horse stood several yards away. "What did you say to him?"

"Nothing that wasn't deserved," the Wormling said. "He needs to be a team player as we undertake our next mission."

"Which is?"

"The Sword of the Wormling. I must have it back. And I think I know how to get it."

They climbed a narrow path along rock walls, but Watcher stopped suddenly when she looked down from the high perch to where the Wormling had killed the sentry. The stick lay in the dirt, but the sentry was gone.

Owen set off toward Diamond-head, knowing deep down that's where the transport flyers had taken the prisoners. Without Watcher to warn him of invisibles, he was at their mercy, a dot on the horizon in the lengthy desert—and, of course, without his sword or *The Book of the King*.

After a night trip across the sand and a rest through the morning, Owen wandered out of the desert and found trees and foliage to block him from view. The weather had turned chilly—certainly not as cold as on the White Mountain but cold enough that Owen would rather have walked in the sunshine than the shade. He recited verses from *The Book of the King* and longed to be with his friends again. He also wished he didn't have to carry the heavy weapons, but he didn't know what he might face. He vowed he would never again surrender his sword, if only he could get it back.

Owen wondered if there was also a Sword of the Son, and if so, what magical powers it might have.

On the second day he came within sight of the mountain that sloped to a peak in a perfect diamond shape, flat on the front and sparkling like glass. The square cast a long shadow on the valley, but when the sun hit it just right, Owen had to shield his eyes from the glare.

At the bottom of the square, several large beasts were being led inside the mouth of a cave, but Owen was too far away to determine whether any humans were present. Only as he drew nearer and began running did he hear people's cries waft over the countryside as they were herded and prodded like animals. Was there no end to the cruelty of the Dragon's forces?

When a horn sounded, Owen feared he had been seen. He dived among rocks and dug a gash in his elbow. He held his breath, waiting for someone or something to pounce. When he peered out again, people were being led to pens while others trudged into the mine.

The Dragon's taskmasters at this mine mouth were unlike

any he had ever seen—long, scaly creatures with dinosaur-like snouts, sharp teeth, and spindly arms that looked like they couldn't pick up a package of noodles. But what they lacked in their arms they made up for with their tails. They swung them at will and sent people flying.

Above the noise came a piercing yell from the mouth of the cave. Owen spotted a pitiful man covered with grime being dragged. A beast tossed him over the pen without opening the gate, and a woman gathered him in her arms.

Owen recognized the pair and knew them well. He was plotting the best route up the steep slope when something moved behind him.

The Changeling

The Changeling had fooled
Watcher thus far, pretending to
be the Wormling and leading her to
a rendezvous with destiny—no doubt
a meeting with the Dragon where she
would be forced to tell everything she
knew before he roasted her in one
fiery breath and devoured her and the
horse.

The Changeling's problem was that
every time an invisible came near,
Watcher sensed it and warned him,
which made him have to duck into
a cave or inside a hollow log or any
number of dreadful places to keep up
the ruse.

Nothing was as bad as where he had

come from, of course, locked in a rock vault by that invisible Nicodemus. The Changeling would make him pay. He had become a horse and tried to kick his way out of the rocky prison, but he cracked a hoof. Then he'd become a mouse and tried to crawl through a small crack in the wall, then an insect, but he made it no farther than as a mouse. He turned himself into a burrowing animal but chipped a front tooth trying to dig out.

It had taken him days to recall the fears of a village child he had once met. The Changeling, able to sense the fears and dreams of those near, had caught the child's vision of a rock monster. Fists of rock, feet of rock, a head of glistening stone, and a body of boulders so strong that as he threw himself against the wall again and again, he finally broke through.

While catching his breath—not easy for a rock monster— he had recognized Watcher's voice and had just enough time to turn himself into the Wormling. Now he was sure to be on the Dragon's most-honored list for having lured this innocent back into the clutches of the king of evil.

The long-winded Watcher talked incessantly, but that was all the better for the Changeling. The more she talked, the less he had to, giving him fewer chances to slip and reveal his true identity.

He had used the opportunity of the sentry finding them to prove his trustworthiness. Quickly conspiring with the thing to fake its death by catching the stick under its wing and dropping to the ground, the Changeling had instructed the creature to summon the Dragon and tell him to meet them at the Castle of the Pines—one of his favorite haunts in the Lowlands. Now all he had to do was keep the ruse going and persuade Watcher to go there.

The horse kept sniffing at the Changeling's clothing— was this a horse or a hound dog? The Changeling suddenly stopped.

"What is it?" Watcher said, looking around.

He reached and felt something moving under the fur on her back. *Good, that chomping little worm is with her,* he thought.

"I have the perfect plan for luring the Dragon into the open and getting my sword back," the Changeling said.

"How will that help us find the Son?" Watcher said. "I mean, I want you to retrieve your sword, but our main task is finding the Son; is it not?"

He patted her head. "You are perceptive, my friend." *A little too perceptive. I'd like to become the Dragon myself and swallow you, but he would not like that.* "After some thought and rumination, I believe the key to finding the Son is tricking the Dragon into telling us where he is."

"What part of the book led you to that?"

The horse whinnied.

The Changeling scowled and opened the book randomly, running his finger along the page as if reading. "When you've lost the sharp thing and you can't find the other, go to the Castle of the Pines." He looked up. "It was here all along."

"I don't remember anything like that," Watcher said. "Let me see."

The Changeling laughed. "What are you going to do, read it to me?"

"Well, you taught me yourself. And the Scribe really helped me grow."

A Watcher had mastered reading? What would the Dragon say about this new wrinkle? All the more reason to get them together. And how would the Dragon feel about the Scribe apparently regaining his mental faculties? The old man had been allowed to go home as a blithering idiot. What strange powers did the Wormling have that could restore such a broken man?

The Changeling closed the book quickly. "Well, I'm glad to hear the words of the King are being spread to the masses. Now let's get going."

The sky turned cloudy and rain fell. Soon snow began to swirl around them.

"Why don't you ride Humphrey?" Watcher said. "It would be easier."

"Yes, but we're not always called to do what is easiest, are we?" The Changeling believed he regained her confidence with that, and he was glad to avoid having to ride the horse. Though that would be better than walking, he was afraid Humphrey was on to him and might throw him.

24

Inner Bees

Connor fell into his wife's arms, and others helped drag him toward the fire. His arms were tired from digging, his legs felt like the bare branches of a dead tree, and his body was covered in mud.

"Are you all right, my darling?" Dreyanna said.

He groaned, unable to answer. How he had survived at the hands of these beasts he didn't know. A seething rage built within him. Perhaps it was the death of his father, perhaps his failure to rescue those he loved. Whatever the reason, his body housed a million bees ready to swarm, though his wife and friends restrained him.

"Bring him water," Dreyanna said.

A young boy handed Connor a wooden ladle, studying his face.

"What are you staring at?" Connor mumbled, his wet, stringy hair hanging in his eyes.

"Nothing, sir," the boy said, eyes wide.

Connor looked him over, a tender young lad, full of life and yet as spent and dirty as the rest of them. The Dragon's workers used the young ones for some of the most dangerous work, crawling and digging at impossible angles, reaching into crevices where snakes or any manner of animal might have burrowed.

Clearly frightened by Connor's look, the boy ran to his mother.

"You're upsetting the children, Connor," Dreyanna said.

"They upset me," he said. "They should be running and playing, catching butterflies and skipping stones, not crawling into dark caverns to do the Dragon's bidding."

"You must not cause more trouble, Connor. They'll kill you."

"They're going to kill us anyway!"

"There's still hope."

"Face it, Dreyanna. The King is not coming back. And neither are those we thought he sent to help us."

Dreyanna leaned close. "You told me to take it a day at a time and wait for the plan to unfold. We must hold on—"

"I'm done holding on," Connor spat, straining to sit up. "And I'm going to take as many of these beasts with me as possible."

Connor struggled to his feet and glared at the two guards at the front of the pen. The commander, a burly creature twice Connor's size, stood on a precipice overlooking the valley. To his left a scrawny guard Connor had never seen before was draped with animal skins against the cold. He seemed to skulk at the edges of the pen as if in hiding, peering into the mouth of the cave.

"Forward guard!" the commander yelled. "Report!"

A chill wind blew and a crow cawed, and again the commander called for his forward guard. He ordered one of the pen guards to search the valley. "He's probably found something to eat."

Meanwhile the scrawny guard was talking to the young boy. The lad nodded and ran to Connor.

"The guard," he whispered, "told me to tell you to make a commotion. He says you know him and that you should trust him." The boy looked at the ground and winced. "He said to do it in memory of your father."

Rage overtook Connor as he charged the front gate, yelling. He thrashed at anyone who tried to restrain him and hit the gate with such force that it nearly came off its hinges. When a guard tried hitting him with a stick, Connor grabbed it and rained blows on the guard.

"Subdue him!" the commander shouted.

The scrawny guard opened the gate and jumped atop Connor, who thrashed more but finally went limp.

"I'll deal with this rabble!" the guard said.

"No!" Dreyanna screamed.

Connor winked at her as he was led out of the pen and up the hill toward the mouth of the cave.

Make it sound good, Connor," Owen said, ripping a leather belt from his disguise and striking it against a rock. The leather made an awful sound, and Connor screamed in agony.

"What are you doing here?" Connor said. "We don't need your help."

"You don't, eh? No, it looks like you're doing quite well. You have a knack for getting thrown into the pens."

"We're organizing a revolt," Connor said, then yelped again as Owen smacked the strap against the wall of the cave.

Owen narrowed his eyes at Connor.

"Come now. You're starving and weak. The beasts watch your every move. They keep you in the mines until you nearly drop. And still you think you can overcome them in your own power?"

With dull eyes, Connor stared at Owen. When the strap struck the wall, he didn't cry out. "What about you? Do you not hold out the same hope? And yet you are alone."

That Connor was even alive was a miracle. But Owen needed him in his fight against the Dragon.

"I've found the Son," Owen said finally.

Like a cat slowly waking by his owner's caress, Connor came to life. "Where?"

"At the Castle on the Moor. I don't have time to explain, but I need you with the army."

Connor looked past Owen. "So the Dragon didn't slaughter him like the beasts said? You've actually seen him?"

"From as close as you are to me. Maybe closer."

"What does he look like? Is he strong? Is he like the King? My father told me the Son would one day return, but I didn't believe him. I thought we were the only army to fight the Dragon."

"We won't force anyone," Owen said. "Only those who are willing to fight should join us. But you must call everyone and bid them to come."

Connor's hollow eyes now shone with a glimmer Owen assumed was hope.

"I must go to the Highlands," Owen said. "The portal must be breached again for the prophecy from *The Book of the King* to be fulfilled."

Connor stared at the floor and finally looked up. "I've always doubted you. Doubted not only who you say you are but your mission."

"My mission is simply to serve the King and do his bidding. And his bidding for you is to help assemble an army to come against the Dragon. Will you do it?"

"If it meant fighting the enemy of my father and our people, I would gather stones for the fight."

Owen smiled. Outside the cave came a wailing cry. "They've discovered the beast I hurt. We must go."

"What did you do to him?" Connor said. "How did you disable him?"

"They are vulnerable here," Owen said, pointing to his own throat. "Catch them there with a sharp jab, they double over, and you can render them senseless."

Connor started for the opening.

Owen held on to him. "The Queen. Is she here?"

Connor's face fell. "They took her away."

"Where?"

"Why are you so interested in the Queen? I thought you were to go back to the Highlands."

"I must know where they've taken her."

A horn sounded and Connor turned away. "They said they would kill 50 of us each time we so much as attacked a guard. How many will they kill if that guard is dead?"

"They won't kill any," Owen said. "I'll help you. But tell me where the Queen is."

Something came scampering from deeper in the cave, so Owen pulled Connor back into the shadows. When a lone guard emerged from the darkness, Owen slung the leather strap around the beast's neck and jerked it off its feet.

Connor leaped onto the animal, and a sharp blow to the neck with a rock rendered it unconscious. Connor drew the rock high over his head for a killing blow, but Owen stopped him. "Enough. Let's free the others."

The Changeling led Watcher and the horse on a zigzag path toward the castle, ever closer to what he hoped was their rendezvous with death. The Changeling could hardly control his glee. He imagined a ceremony in his honor, the Dragon hanging a medal around his neck, applause from the army horde. The Dragon would no doubt offer him a seat at the council table, and he could go from court jester to one of the master's most trusted aides.

Several times the Watcher dragged him under cover when invisibles flew over. Why did they keep looking for him after he had requested a meeting at the castle? Perhaps the Dragon didn't trust him. Or more likely the invisibles had merely been sent as insurance against another slip with someone as important as the Watcher. The Dragon didn't want the Watcher to escape.

When they reached the huge lake within view of the castle, Watcher asked if the Wormling could remember the last time they were here.

"Of course," the Changeling said. "What was your favorite part of that trip?"

"Favorite?" Watcher said. "We were nearly killed, and Quamay was. I don't even want to think about it."

The Changeling tried to recall the type of drivel the Wormling would say in such a situation. "Yes, but many times good things happen when negative occurrences happen too."

"You mean like *The Book of the King* says?" Watcher said, closing her eyes and reciting, "'Celebrate difficulties, because if you endure them, you will learn patience.'"

The Changeling rolled his eyes. "Exactly. Fighting the Dragon will make us stronger."

"If it doesn't kill us first," Watcher muttered.

The Changeling laughed. "Yes. Yes, that's very funny."

They came upon a wooded thicket that evening, and snow began falling heavily. Using the shelter of the trees, they made a refuge, and the Changeling gathered food for the horse and Watcher. "Wait right here while I find something for me to eat."

"I sense invisibles nearby," Watcher said.

"I will be safe," the Changeling said.

"But—"

"Stop!" he said. "I'll be fine. Stay here and keep our refuge warm."

He stole away, making sure the Watcher didn't follow, and moved to the frigid waters of the lake. Carefully he slipped in, feet and hands changing into large fins. In the form of a long fish now, he quickly swam toward the castle. When an animal approached, the Changeling sounded an underwater warning and scared it away.

Finally he flopped onto the ground and quickly grew wings and a scaly back. Still dripping, he rose through the falling snow to the parapet and entered the Dragon's chamber. It was empty, though a fresh scent of smoke told him the Dragon was not far away.

RHM met the Changeling, and they exchanged pleasantries. "We must keep our voices down," RHM said. "His Highness is already in bed. Let's move onto the balcony."

The Changeling grabbed rancid fruit from a bowl and followed, pointing out the general location of Watcher and the horse.

"Why don't you let us bring them in?" RHM said. "You'll still have your reward, and we'll have the prize in hand."

"Oh no. No one else delivers my prize. Will His High-Hot-Breath be here in the morning?"

"Yes, up and waiting for you."

"Good. I'll have them here in time for his breakfast."

Owen freed his friends from the pen, but instead of running they hobbled like old people. Owen and Connor and several of the strongest men jumped the guards, using Owen's technique of attacking them in the neck and rendering them unconscious. They did the same to the guards posted deep inside the mine. The workers there, mostly children and younger women, followed them out.

Hundreds stood, watching Owen. "Is this everyone?" he said.

Connor nodded. "Now what do we do? If we don't kill these guards, they'll alert the invisibles that come by each morning."

"How often are jewels shipped out?" Owen said.

"Once a week. Tomorrow is the next shipment."

The crowd looked hungry, thirsty, and ready to drop. Owen found himself too emotional to look into the faces of the children and moved back into the cave.

Connor soon followed. "Why did you leave?"

Owen found it difficult to even talk. "They are like animals without anyone to tend to their needs. They remind me of . . ."

"Who?"

"Of myself. In the other world I had a father, but he paid very little attention to me. I was on my own much of the time and without guidance. Still . . ."

A torch flickered near the entrance. Connor stayed in the shadows. "Yes?"

"I felt a strange sense of direction, something moving me forward." Owen sighed. "I sure wish your father were here with us."

Connor clenched his teeth. "I don't know if I can ever forgive you for your part in his death. But if you can help save these people and get us out of here, I will fight beside you."

Owen put a hand on Connor's shoulder. "The battle will come soon enough."

"Go out and encourage them," Connor said. "They need to hear from you."

Employing the strongest of the group and two-wheeled carts, they managed to move the knocked-out guards into the cave. Two were waking, but Connor quickly put them out again. Owen took their cloaks and animal skins.

Owen found a stash of explosives and carefully lit the powdered fuse, running down the hill before a terrific blast rocked the mountain and sealed the mouth of the cave. The prisoners cheered, and Owen herded them into their pen (in case an invisible flew past), then helped prepare a meal.

Owen and some others dressed as the guards and even imitated them, dragging their feet and ordering people about. The children giggled so much it was hard for them to eat. Owen could tell it had been a long time since they had laughed.

From inside the cave they heard the guards waking and yelling. Connor stood by, but no one really believed the guards could dig their way out.

Owen and the other leaders agreed on a strategy. Seeing the fear in the young ones' eyes, he told them a story that made them laugh so hard they cried. Even the adults held their sides, eyes dancing.

"And now let me tell you another story," Owen said, "of a King who had a Son who was taken. The King loved him so much that he decided to rescue him. But not in the usual way, with swords blazing and soldiers storming a castle. No, this was much quieter, with much less fanfare."

"How did he do it?" a child said, eyes wide, as if she were waiting to unwrap a birthday present.

"He spoke," Owen said. "He told a story. And the words rescued the Son."

"How could words rescue anyone?" a father said.

"That makes no sense," a mother said.

"Ah, but you don't understand the words or the heart of the one who spoke them. Words are powerful. They can mean death or they can mean freedom for the same person."

"Magical words?" the child said.

"In a way," Owen said. "But not magic that's stirred in a potion or casts a spell. This is a bottomless magic filled with love, one you can't understand until it overtakes you—until you abandon yourself to it."

The parents listened with skeptical faces, but the children sat spellbound.

"The love you speak about," a boy said. "It is only for the Son in your story, right?"

Owen smiled. "That's what I used to believe. But the more I have learned of this love, the more I understand that it's available to each of us." He stood and looked over the crowd. "The King's Son is coming back. Perhaps he is here."

The people looked at each other and seemed to marvel at the story.

In the flickering firelight of the camp, people appeared to sleep peacefully, probably unafraid for the first time since they'd been led here. With the soft breathing of the children and the noisier snoring of the adults, Owen went to Connor. Dreyanna slept with her head on her husband's shoulder.

"The Queen," Owen whispered, "where did they take her?"

Connor looked away and rubbed his eyes. "I overheard guards say the Dragon feared the Son might return for his mother. She was taken alone, and we have not heard from her since. The guards did not even seem to know the destination.

"What does this mean for you?" Connor said. "Will you go with us?"

Owen nodded. "As far as the White Mountain."

Watcher was awakened by the
Wormling before dawn, and
she and Humphrey followed him, setting out for the castle. Several inches
of snow had fallen, so they left tracks,
making Watcher pine for her home in
the mountains.

She knew what the townspeople,
especially the children, said about
her—that she was strange to keep the
ancient tradition of waiting for the
Wormling. Still, she had waited and
watched. And now as she walked by
his side, warmth coursed through her.
She had proved them all wrong and

distinguished herself by her diligence. She wondered if anyone dared scoff at her anymore.

"Isn't the countryside beautiful?" the Wormling said. "Like
someone threw a blanket over it while we slept."

"You didn't sleep," Watcher said. "I heard you pacing the
whole night."

"Probably something I ate," he said. "I can't wait to get my
sword back. Can you imagine having all three with us again—
the sword, the book, and the Mucker?"

"You will be ready to go back to the Highlands," Watcher
said. "After you've located the Son, of course."

The Wormling stopped. "What did you say?" He looked
pained, as though he had lost a dear relative.

"You've said all along that you need to go back to the
Highlands," Watcher said. "I assumed when you had everything, you would do that."

"Of course. How perceptive of you. Hurry along now."

Humphrey whinnied, and the Wormling shushed him.
"We're getting close to the castle."

The moon was still high, occasionally peeking from a
shroud of clouds like a child playing a game.

Across the immense body of water, the castle loomed
dark and foreboding and sent shivers down Watcher's flanks.
Strange that the Wormling could stride so resolutely toward

it without fear. He didn't even seem to remember much about the last time they'd been here.

Humphrey whinnied when the surface of the water swirled and became choppy as if something huge had just passed below. Or was it following them?

Watcher heard wings and looked up, expecting a demon flyer, but it was just a bird.

The Wormling swatted at it and kept moving, clearly eager to reach the castle before first light.

Watcher had never seen the Wormling swat at a fly before. He must be preoccupied.

As they passed through another wooded area, Humphrey blew air through his lips and shook his tail.

"What?" Watcher asked. "Do you see something?"

But just as Humphrey's eyes fixed on Watcher, the Wormling turned. "Come on, you two. Keep up."

With the castle rising before them like a ghost, the three walked single file near the lake. "Watch your step here," the Wormling said. "The water is frigid."

As the Wormling grabbed a sapling and pulled himself up the bank, Watcher heard a splash and turned to see Humphrey sinking into the water and great jaws coming after her as well.

In a flash, she was yanked into the freezing lake with the horse, and they were pulled deep into the shadows.

The sky was still dark when Owen moved the others into position at the camp. The people plainly would rather have stayed asleep, as this was the first time they'd been well fed, but they obeyed. Connor, as the largest among them, took the commander's place on a high rock. With the man's animal skins and spear, he looked frighteningly similar. The question was, could he and the rest fool the demon flyers?

Owen wished Watcher were here to warn them of demon flyers. Connor held up a finger to signal that one demon flyer had landed. (There was dust flying everywhere and large talon marks in the ground.) The demon flyer would lead the two transport flyers in the distance.

Owen and the others pretended to berate and punish the prisoners, slinging leather straps and shaking weapons at them. The people cowered on cue.

Two transport flyers arrived with the rising sun, wings flapping slowly, a cage suspended beneath each of them.

Connor imitated the guards, shouting, "Bring the prisoners for loading!"

Owen positioned several men before the pile of mined rocks and jewels.

Then came an unearthly voice sounding like grating metal. "Why is the cave closed?" the demon flyer said.

"Trouble with some of the beasts," Connor said. "We've sealed them until they die."

"The Dragon will be displeased," the flyer roared. "We are near the quota."

"This load completes the quota," Connor said. "Go and tell him."

"I accompany the transport!"

"You think those beasts don't know the way? Take the news to the Dragon now! You will no doubt earn a reward of food and drink."

The transport flyers landed, lowering the cages.

Owen slapped his leather strap against a rock near the head of a prisoner. "Get to work!"

The wind rose quickly as the demon flyer left.

Connor held out a hand as if to say, "Keep working until it is out of sight."

Finally he stood. "Everyone into the cages!"

Owen opened the cage doors, and the transport flyers inched back, plainly sensing something amiss.

The people hesitated, murmuring, and children wept.

"It's all right," Owen said. "Don't be frightened. Everything will be okay. Just get inside as quick as you can. We're taking you to safety."

Connor rushed to Owen's side, whispering, "What if they take us back to the Dragon?"

"It is written," Owen said, "'He will have charge over the beasts of the land, sea, and air. He will bid them come, and they will obey.'"

"Who is 'he'?" Connor said. "The Wormling?"

"You'll learn," Owen said. "Soon enough."

Connor and his wife crawled into a cage together, leading others inside. Owen ushered people into the other cage. When all were inside, both cages were full to overflowing. Owen closed the doors and secured them so no one would fall out. One flyer began to flap its wings, but Owen commanded it to stop, and to everyone's amazement—even Owen's—it did.

Owen tied a long piece of rope to the neck of one transport flyer as the beast eyed him warily and edged back, tipping the cage. The people cried out, but Owen calmed the beast by petting it like a dog and talking soothingly to it.

Owen tied the other end of the rope to the foot of the other flyer, then crawled up its back and wrapped his arms around its neck.

Just like riding Humphrey, Owen thought. *Except Humphrey doesn't fly or weigh 8,000 pounds.*

Owen dug in with his heels, and the flyer rose into the air with a jerk, pulling the cage quickly from the ground. Immediately the second flyer was yanked aloft. Owen felt the same sensation as when he rose in a fast elevator in a tall building in his Highland town. The transport flyer's muscles rippled and swelled under him.

Children squealed with delight, as if on an amusement park ride, certainly different from when Owen had flown here before. Adults kept them from the edges of the cage, just in case.

The flyers rose to cloud level, heading into the golden sunlight, and the temperature dropped. The beasts were trained to fly from the mines to the Dragon, but Owen steered his flyer toward the White Mountain in the distance. The following flyer tried to veer off, but the rope tightened and it was forced to follow.

Owen pulled an animal skin over his shoulders and hunkered down to stay warm.

Watcher gasped and swallowed freezing water as she plunged to the depths. Only when she finally saw the lights of the underground cavern did she believe she might survive. They broke the surface in the jaws of the huge crocodile, and Humphrey sputtered and shook his way onto the rocky shore. Coughing, Watcher examined *The Book of the King* and found it and Mucker in good condition. She had fashioned a waterproof pouch out of jargid skins for the book and was glad.

"Rotag!" she exulted. "Great to see you, but what about the Wormling?"

"A thousand pardons, my friend,"

Rotag said, his voice gravelly. "We tried to think of some other way—"

"We?"

Humphrey stepped back and whinnied as Batwing flew in.

"Are they all right?" Batwing said in his high-pitched voice. "Were you noticed?"

"How could we not be?" Rotag said. "We made quite a splash."

"What's going on?" Watcher said.

"That is not the Wormling you were with," Batwing said. "Tusin spotted it last night headed for the castle, and I overheard its conversation with an aide of the Dragon."

Humphrey whinnied and struck a hoof to the ground.

"You were trying to tell me," Watcher said.

"The one you think is the Wormling is actually a Changeling," Batwing said. "He was luring you to the castle to be food for the Dragon."

Watcher shook her head. "But why couldn't I sense he was not the Wormling?"

A small creature climbed down into the light.

"Tusin!" Watcher said.

The two hugged, and Tusin patted her on the back. "We thought it was the Wormling at first as well, but Batwing learned the truth." He sighed. "My guess is that somewhere inside you, there was a feeling that something was wrong, out of place. But you ignored that."

"I was so happy to see him," Watcher said. "I wanted it to be him."

"Yes," Tusin said. "And that is why it is important to never ignore those feelings. No matter who it is who gives them to you."

"We were going to be eaten?" Watcher said.

"After the whereabouts of the real Wormling were tortured from you," Batwing said.

"Never," Watcher said. "All I can say is thank you." She introduced Humphrey and told him, "This is the hall of meeting I told you of, and these are our friends. Without them, we would never have escaped the Dragon."

Rotag asked about the Wormling, and Watcher told him everything she knew, which wasn't much. Then she put a hand over her mouth. "Oh, Humphrey, what if he comes back for us, and we're not there?"

The horse shook his head and nickered.

"Perhaps we can help," Rotag said. "What did the Changeling say was the reason you were going to the castle?"

"He said we were going to fetch the Sword of the Wormling."

Rotag cleared his throat and nodded at Tusin, who stood and held his head high. "Meeting of the assembly convenes on this day of the King, all members present, the honorable Rotag presiding, the honored Watcher and Humphrey as guests. The matter of the friends of the Wormling is the agenda."

Peril

The Dragon paced the library, which ironically held no books, for he had banned and burned them long ago. As he passed the empty shelves, he gloated. He had kept words and knowledge from the people of the Lowlands these many years, and soon the Highlands would experience the same—though they had no idea what was about to happen.

The Dragon had been awakened just before sunlight by a demon flyer's report that the final mineral load was on its way from Diamondhead. That, coupled with the prospect of questioning the Wormling's Watcher one final time, had left the scaly beast as sleepless as a child awaiting Christmas morning. Watcher was the channel to the Wormling, and the Wormling was the channel to the Son, and the death of the Son meant the end of the King's plan for this world and the other.

The Dragon rubbed his claws in glee. He let out a screaming belch of fire that scorched the shelves.

RHM entered quickly, rubbing his eyes and yawning. "Yes, Highness?"

"What have you heard from the Changeling? He should be here by now."

RHM shook his head as if trying to knock cobwebs from his brain. "Stalkers guarding the outer wall will let us know the moment they approach."

"And the flyer from Diamondhead? Have you rewarded it for its report?"

"Absolutely. It sits even now in the dining hall devouring the remains of whatever you killed yesterday."

"Whatever or whoever?" the Dragon said, chuckling. He looked outside at the gathering light. "A pity that day comes so soon. How I love when darkness envelops and grips the land. People are more afraid in the dark—did you know that?"

RHM nodded. "Their teeth chatter, and their eyes widen when you prowl—"

"Oh, stop it!" the Dragon roared, enraptured, eyes twinkling. "It makes me want to go burn a village right now. Or

at least scatter some sheep and eat a small shepherd or two."
He licked his lips and snorted. "And maybe swoop down on a
few of the runners—you know, the ones who scurry from the
villages and try to make it to the tree line? That's one of my
favorite pastimes."

"Your specialty, sire."

The Dragon sighed. "I will do greater works than those,
my friend. The big show isn't far away now. Once we refine
the last of the precious stones and get them to the White
Mountain, we make the world anew—into what it was meant
to be."

"I only hope that one day I might be—"

"As powerful as I?"

"Well, that's too much to dream. But close."

The Dragon studied his front claws and rolled his eyes. "You
may aspire to greatness, RHM. You may imitate, but there is
only one of me. And there will be only one nest of offspring."

"Offspring?"

"How could that have escaped from my mouth? I expect
you to keep that slip of the tongue to yourself."

"But, sire, what—?"

Footsteps in the hallway ended with a light tap on the
door. The Dragon beckoned with a booming voice, and a
timid creature with shaking limbs walked in. He lowered his
head respectfully, and the Dragon roared at him.

"Begging your pardon, sire, but there's a matter of great importance I thought you would—"

A horn sounded outside, and the tiny beast seemed to nearly wet himself.

The Dragon pointed a sharpened talon at him. "Wait here."

With RHM in tow, the Dragon strode down the hall, through the bedroom, and onto the parapet overlooking the water.

Just below, the horn blower ducked when he saw the Dragon. "Sorry to disturb you, Highness. Someone approaches from the wood."

The Dragon saw a speck in the distance, limping toward the castle. "RHM, what is that?"

The aide gasped. "I believe it's the Changeling, sire."

Not long later they helped the battered and bruised Changeling into the castle. He coughed and sputtered.

"Where are your prisoners?" the Dragon demanded.

"Do not spare me, O great one," the Changeling said. "I have failed you and your magnificent kingdom. The Watcher beguiled me with stories, and when I least expected it, she and the horse descended on me with a fierceness I have seldom seen. I had no chance even to turn myself into something else. She bit and scratched and clawed, and the horse kicked me until I was as bruised as a month-old banana."

"How did they find you out?" the Dragon said, seething.

The Changeling lolled his head. "Oh, I can't say any more. Please just turn me to ash, O great one. I deserve it."

"Yes, you do. A painful death."

"Make me writhe," the Changeling said.

RHM moved back, clearly fearing the inevitable blast.

But the Dragon leaned closer and studied the Changeling's bruises. "I would rather you live and serve me with your special talents than pay such a terrible price."

The Changeling's eyes snapped open as if he had just realized it was his birthday. "Ask me for anything, and I will do it."

The Dragon's muscles tensed. "How long ago did they elude you?"

"Not long. They can't be far. I came as quickly as I could."

The Dragon shot into the air, plainly forgetting the parapet's stone arch. Banging it sent debris flying. "Find them! Send every available being, and do not fail me this time!"

The Changeling sprang up and ran outside, ordering flyers and searchers to follow.

The Dragon returned to the stairway, where the timid creature stood. "Now, what was important enough for you to disturb us?"

Trembling, he said, "The transport flyers have not arrived with the load of gems, O revered one."

"What? They should have arrived long ago! RHM, fetch me the demon flyer."

"We have reports," the shaking guard added, "that two transport flyers were seen heading north. No demon flyer accompanied the shipment, but there were prisoners in the cages."

"Prisoners?" the Dragon repeated.

"Yes, and the report said it looked like a human rode on the back of one of the transport flyers."

RHM returned with the demon flyer—invisible to humans but not to the Dragon and his underlings. This flyer bore smallish wings, long fangs and talons, and a belly so full of food and drink that it could hardly stand. When it walked, it sloshed like a bucket of water. It saluted and nearly toppled. "It is my pleasure to serve you," the flyer managed, then belched.

The Dragon took a soothing tone. "Who told you the mining was complete?"

"One of the guards."

"What did he look like?"

"The usual, sire. Animal skins, gruff voice, and to tell the truth, I wasn't paying much attention. I was so excited to—"

"It is your job to pay attention," the Dragon boomed.

The demon flyer immediately dropped to his knees, as if he knew what was coming.

"Did the guard tell you to make haste and come tell me the good news? Or was that your idea?"

"His, sire. I—I didn't want to—to leave the convoy, b-but he insisted, assuring me you would b-be pl-pleased, so—"

"So pleased that I would offer you your weight in food and drink. Is that it?"

"No, sire. I simply wanted—"

Molten fire shot from the Dragon's mouth and enveloped the poor creature. All watching turned away, except the Dragon, who delighted in the fireworks. He coughed, swallowed, and turned to the window, where daylight streamed in with great intensity. "This has the Wormling written all over it. If the miners have been freed, he gathers an army."

"That is nothing to you," RHM said. "What good is that pip-squeak without his sword and without the Son he's been seeking?"

The Dragon's eyes drooped and then shot back and forth, as if he were computing some long math problem. "Perhaps he prepares the army for the Son's return. Or worse, perhaps he has found the Son."

The Dragon scratched his back and turned to go upstairs. The timid creature cowered in the corner as he passed.

"The passage in that infernal book," he wheezed. "What did it say?"

"Which, sire?" RHM said.

The Dragon's eyes drooped and then shot back and forth, as if he were computing some long math problem. "This is all about the King's Son. Perhaps the Wormling prepares the army for the Son's return."

The Dragon muttered something he had read in *The Book of the King*—at least something that had stuck in his head but his heart could not understand. He turned to RHM. "Our task is simple. If we can keep the Wormling from returning to the Highlands and finding this Son, any threat against me will be gone. All we must do is kill the Wormling."

While Watcher met and planned with Rotag and Tusin, Batwing left on a spying trip to the castle. He returned after a long while with word that while the Sword of the Wormling was not there, he had overheard wonderful news about the Wormling himself. Batwing told of his possibly being spotted on his way to the White Mountain.

Watcher couldn't help but be overjoyed. "He must have been caught somehow, thrown in with the others, and found a way to escape."

"It does sound like the nature of the Wormling," Tusin said. "But why would he be going in the direction of the White Mountain?"

"Perhaps he has discovered where the Son is," Rotag said.

"We have friends near the White Mountain," Watcher said. "I must go there at once."

"It is a long journey," Batwing said, "even for me. By the time you arrive, the Dragon would have been there and gone."

"Is there some other way?" Watcher said.

Tusin tapped his lower lip with a claw and paced. "Perhaps."

Rotag glanced at him. "I hope you're not thinking what I think you're thinking."

Tusin looked up. "You know he is sorry for what he did—"

"He betrayed us and the King," Rotag snapped. "He is the reason many died at the hands of the Dragon and why we must meet in secret."

"Who?" Watcher said.

Tusin sat near her and leaned forward, paws on his knees. "Many seasons ago, four of us pledged allegiance to the King and vowed to stand against the Dragon. The fourth was Machree, a flyer with a great wingspan."

"But not much sense," Rotag mumbled.

"Somehow the Dragon or his followers got him to reveal the location of our council. Many died."

"What happened to Machree?" Watcher said.

"He took the blood money and flew away," Rotag said.

"He lives in the Great Forest," Tusin said, "one of the King's favorite places. He loved to walk there in the early morning."

"It might take days to find him," Rotag said. "And besides, I am totally against this."

"I could find him and have him here within the hour," Batwing said.

Rotag rolled his eyes and shook his great head.

"It's worth the risk," Watcher said. "Please find him, Batwing. And hurry."

Owen's transport flyer raced into
the teeth of a strong, biting
wind, so he steered it lower to warmer
air. He could tell the huddled people
in the cages were freezing.

Everything in Owen screamed that
he should find the Queen and release
her, yet *The Book of the King* made
clear that the next prophecy to fulfill
was that he return to the Highlands.

The time of the Son draws near.
When the Wormling has accomplished the breach of the four
portals of the Dragon, prepare
the way for the armies of the
King. Let every kindred, tongue,

and tribe of the Lowlands ready themselves for battle, for the time of the Great Stirring has begun. And this stirring will lead to the Final Union of the Son and his bride. Rejoice and be exceedingly glad when the signs point to his return.

Owen let the words wash over him anew. How he wished he could read *The Book of the King* front to back—including the missing chapter—with the new knowledge that he himself was the Son. But why were there blank pages in the back? He had never read the end of the battle with the Dragon. It was shrouded in mysterious language. Had he missed a prophecy?

A cry came from the cage beneath the other flyer, not of fear but delight. The clouds dissolved to reveal splendor in the distance. The White Mountain rose, majestic and brilliant, the sun glinting off its snowcapped slopes, golden and white against a dazzling blue sky. *I wish Watcher could see this*, Owen thought, nearly choking up.

As they drew closer, the transport flyers dipped and jerked through wind swells like skiffs on the waves near the islands of Mirantha.

Owen guided them past the villages at the base of the mountain. Mothers and fathers called for children in snow-covered fields, and the kids stared and waved as they passed.

They rose through the pass where vaxors had attacked

them, and Owen shuddered at the memory of how far Humphrey had jumped from the precipice.

Why had the King entrusted Owen with this responsibility? Had the King given him power he hadn't tapped into yet? What rights might he have as the Son that he didn't know or understand?

Though Owen wanted to know everything now, he knew he would not have been able to handle it all at once. Had he been told back at the bookstore every detail of his journey, he'd surely have given up before he started. First he had to come to believe he was the Wormling. Now he had to accept the responsibility of being the Son. Knowing the King's blood coursed through his veins gave him courage and strength. He had never felt like royalty in the bookstore. His father the King had mapped out the plan thus far, and Owen was determined to follow him the rest of the way.

Watcher had the book and Mucker, who was vital to the next stage of Owen's quest. His plan, once he reached Yodom, was to find her in the caves where he had left her. But he had to do this quickly before the Dragon and his cohorts discovered him.

The farther up the mountain he flew, the more he felt as if he were in a shaken snow globe. Huge flakes came sideways, so fast and heavy he couldn't even see the other transport flyer. He just hoped the flyers could sense the mountain and not plow into it.

Owen forced the flyer to descend, and the tether tightened as they fell. Near the ground the flyer flapped faster, hovering and blowing much snow away.

"We'll walk from here," Owen said as he opened the cages. "We can find shelter in a nearby village."

"The people are cold," Connor said. "Let's build a fire and wait out the storm."

Owen pulled Connor out of earshot of the others. "You have a heart of a warrior, but we must work together. Soon you'll be in charge of all these people. I want you as my general to oversee the troops."

"Where are you going?" Connor said.

"I have an important mission in the Highlands. I must again breach the four portals. Then we must prepare for the wedding of the Son and the battle with the Dragon."

"In that order?" Connor said.

Owen closed his eyes and recited from *The Book of the King* the first words he had read from it in the Highlands:

"When the shadows of two worlds collide and the four portals are breached, know that the end of the reign of the evil one is near. Men will bring news of the return of justice and righteousness, along with the return of the Son. What has been two will be made one throughout the land. Make way a path in the wilderness for the Searcher. Open the portal for the Wormling, for he will be armed with the book.

"Let there be rejoicing in every hill and valley, from the tops of the mountains to the depths of the oceans. Let every creature that has breath, on earth and under and over, cry out. Victory is at hand. The shadows will be dispelled, and the Son will return for his bride."

Connor stared at Owen. "So you don't know."

"I'm not sure. Perhaps the war ends before the wedding begins. Perhaps the other way around. The book does not say specifically."

Connor's wife came and whispered, "The women and children are losing feeling in their fingers and toes."

Owen took off his animal skin and gave it to her.

"Prepare the children," Connor told her. "We move up the mountain shortly."

Dreyanna looked at him sharply, but he nodded and she went back to the others.

Owen untied the rope from one transport flyer and smacked its back end, as if to release it. The beast simply looked at him as if it wasn't going anywhere without its companion.

"Maybe they're married," Connor said.

"Maybe they don't want to go back to the Dragon."

Batwing returned to Watcher and
the others with the news that he
had found Machree in the forest, but
the bird would not even listen.

"I told you he was not worth considering," Rotag said.

"Did you tell him the importance of
this mission?" Watcher said.

Batwing nodded. "I tried everything
short of bribery, but he said he knew
the council members were against
him and that he would rather be left
alone."

Watcher looked at the ground. "All
that speed and power and ability. How

can he let that go to waste? To have strength and not use it for the King is—"

"Normal for most," Tusin said. "And understand this about the King: He does not use us because we are strong. He uses us in spite of our weaknesses. We all have something that holds us back. Perhaps our pride. Perhaps some physical difficulty. Lack of intelligence. Slowness of speech. The King uses our faults even more than he uses our strengths."

"What does that have to do with getting me back to the Wormling?" Watcher said.

Rotag cleared his throat. "Perhaps the King has prepared some other way. Or perhaps he does not want you back with the Wormling just now."

"But I have the book. And I have Mucker. He needs these. I sense it with everything in me." She turned to Batwing. "Can you take me to Machree?"

"Much too dangerous," Tusin said.

Rotag huffed. "Out of the question."

"The Dragon's forces would be on you in a second. Batwing can fly under their vision and skirt them, but they would—"

"I have no other choice," Watcher said. "I have to find the Wormling. Batwing, will you take me?"

Batwing looked at the others, then nodded.

Watcher crawled out of the underground cavern muddy and wet, which made her more difficult to spot from the air.

Batwing flew ahead of her, searching for any unfriendlies, while Watcher darted from tree to tree until they came to the Great Forest.

"Wait here," Batwing said.

Watcher hid behind a rock, trying to stay still but mostly shivering and her teeth chattering.

A whoosh above startled her, and she spotted an enormous winged creature heading for her. If Batwing hadn't described Machree beforehand, she would have sworn the bird was from the Dragon.

The wings were multicolored—but mostly brown and white—and the face was that of a hawk with a sharp beak and piercing eyes. "You are the Watcher?" he said, his voice high-pitched.

She nodded. "I've come to plead with you on behalf of the Wormling."

The bird blinked and quickly looked both ways. "Pleading will do you no good."

"You do not wish to help the King?"

"Perhaps if it were the King asking."

"The Wormling represents the King. He is on an important mission from him. I have *The Book of the King* here with me to prove it."

Machree looked down his beak at the book and smirked.

"Why would you want to lug about so many pages full of scribblings?"

"Well, these are the words of the King—"

"The little bat says you have powers. Like what?"

"I'm a Watcher. I can detect invisibles above."

"But not below?"

"Correct. If they are in the water or underground, I do not sense them."

"Well, I live in this forest. I have no need of you or your abilities."

Machree spread his wings, but before he could lift off, Watcher shouted, "I should have known! Tusin was right! He and Rotag said you would not help!"

The bird settled again. "You know those two as well, do you?"

"They helped in a previous skirmish with the Dragon."

"Let them take you where you want to go."

Watcher was desperate to think of what to say next. She couldn't let Machree fly away—she would never reach the Wormling.

"They cannot get me there in time. Besides, I cannot trust them like I can trust you." She had said this to impress and, she hoped, to change the bird's mind. But a strange feeling came over her, as if she had eaten something rotten.

Machree narrowed his eyes. "And what will you offer me?"

"Offer? I have nothing."

"Surely if this Wormling is an agent of the King, he has riches at his disposal."

"I suppose, but I cannot offer what I do not have."

Machree seemed to be thinking. "Intercede for me. Tell the Wormling I helped you on the condition that I become a member of the King's cabinet."

Watcher locked eyes with the bird. "I will if you take me there now."

He knelt and Watcher climbed on his back, but as they rose she still felt uneasy. In fact, she was already filled with regret.

35
Return to Yodom

As Owen and the others trudged through the deep snow toward Yodom, something seemed strange. The path had widened. Tree stumps and rocks had been moved so the transport flyers were able to walk, rather than having to lift themselves over the path with their powerful wings.

As they neared the place that over-looked the town, instead of finding the rock pile the people had used to vanquish the vaxors, there stood small huts and lean-tos. The village had expanded.

"Halt!" A man shrouded in snow held a glowing torch and moved toward them quickly.

Connor drew a weapon he had taken from a guard at the mine.

"Put that away," Owen said.

The man's eyes widened as he took in the size of the crowd before him, especially when one of the transport flyers lifted a wing.

"Sound the alarm!" the man yelled.

"Wait!" Owen said. "We come in peace—"

But it was too late. A ram's horn blew, and the man disappeared into the snowy darkness. Another ram's horn sounded farther away, then another that seemed to echo deep inside the mountain.

"They will kill us," Connor said, again unsheathing his weapon.

"Not when they find out who we are," Owen said, but he turned to face archers with flaming arrows through the haze. A phalanx of warriors with shields knelt before them.

"People of Yodom!" Owen shouted. "This is not the army of the Dragon before you! We have escaped the Dragon!"

"Stand back!" came an older, shaky voice. "Put down your weapons!" A hooded figure made his way through the snow, glancing up at the transport flyers, then locking eyes with Owen.

"Scribe!" Owen shouted.

"Wormling!" the old man said, and they embraced. "Come and warm yourselves at the fellowship cavern. All of you."

The Scribe looked quite different from when Owen had first seen him. His eyes were bright and full of life, and he was smartly dressed and busy with the details of lodging the newcomers.

"Send the families into the back. Children without parents can go with Rachel, and those of fighting age can sleep here—after they have eaten and warmed themselves and found new clothing."

The scene around them was like an old-fashioned homecoming. There was everything but music, and Owen knew Erol and his clan would take care of that when they arrived.

"How did so many get here?" Owen said as the Scribe pulled him aside and set a plate of steaming food before him.

"The news of the escape of the White Mountain prisoners brought many curious people," the Scribe said, pouring hot cider for him. "Most have stayed with us and become protectors, but as you can see, we are almost filled to overflowing."

"And your mind?" Owen said. "It seems clear."

"Never better. My wife can't believe the transformation, and neither can the people of the town. Once a doddering old fool, now I lead this camp as if I were 20. I daresay that friend of yours, Watcher, helped me by remembering so much of *The Book of the King*. When she recited it, I wrote it down, and it

has helped me immensely. I should show you my manuscript.
. . . Did I say something wrong, Wormling? You look—"

"I just miss my friend. I wish she were here with the book
and Mucker." Owen leaned close and whispered to the old
man, "I know this will come as a shock, but we're going to
need many more warriors. Even now, my friend Mordecai and
the clan of Erol are scouring the countryside for volunteers."

"Who would not want to come and fight with you?" the
Scribe said. "Tell me, has your quest been successful? Did you
find the Son?"

Owen smiled. This man had known his father the King
intimately. "Listen," Owen said, but before he could continue,
a scuffle broke out between Connor's men and those watching
the weapons.

"I'll handle this," Owen said.

36

The Plunge

Watcher buried her legs behind Machree's neck and burrowed her face into the swooping bird's soft, warm feathers. The wind whipped at her fur, and she clutched tight *The Book of the King* and hoped Mucker would be all right.

The first few minutes of the flight were the worst, as Machree fought to gain altitude, despite being fat, out of shape, and short of breath.

"Why the White Mountain?" Machree screeched.

"Our friends are there," Watcher said. "How far away are we?"

"Through the night and on into morning," Machree said, breathless and obviously concerned.

"Have you not ventured from the forest since what happened with the council?"

Machree took a long time to answer. "If you were hated by the Dragon and those who follow the King, would you go out? Truth is, I fear both. If the demon flyers catch me, it's over. And I can't bear seeing any of the council, knowing that I . . ."

"What?" Watcher said. "What did you do?"

"Don't make me retell history. Keep your eyes peeled, and alert me to any danger."

Darkness covered the land, but lights twinkled above. The Wormling had explained that some in his world believed the stars were the result of a great explosion. When he told her how many believed things far from what *The Book of the King* taught, she despaired. How glad she would be when they found the King's Son and would be able to attend the wedding. She hoped the Wormling had found the Son, but if he had, that meant he would be traveling back to his world. Would she ever see him again? Would the Son's uniting of the two worlds keep them friends or separate them forever?

A screech pierced the stillness, and Watcher looked up in time to see clouds dispersing. With a sickening thud, something hit Machree from behind, and feathers flew everywhere. She held on desperately as they plunged, hurtling out of control.

Watcher suddenly realized that she was holding Machree so tight with her legs that she had cut off his air. She let up and shouted, "Spread your wings! We're going to crash!"

The wind screamed in her ears as she peered at something on the ground—the reflection of the moon in water. It grew larger as they fell.

Owen awoke to a gorgeous blue sky and a new fluffy, white coating on the ground. The air was crisp, and tree boughs were weighted down with the white stuff.

Owen had separated Connor and the other young men who had quarreled over who would lead the group in battle. "I need your passion and your will," Owen had said, "but I also need you to understand who the enemy is."

Connor had torn away and retreated to Dreyanna. The Scribe wanted Owen to return to their conversation, but Owen told him they would talk again in the morning.

With the sun glaring off the snow

and making him shade his eyes, Owen checked on the transport flyers. They shook off the snow from their backs, and one of them burped.

"So, you're happy to see me?" Owen said, laughing.

The animals swung their tails and shook so much snow onto Owen that he had to shield himself with his hands. "All right, all right, I'm glad to see you as well. I just hope your boss doesn't see you and send a horde of demon flyers."

As if they understood, the flyers hunkered down in the snow and dipped their heads.

"You have a way with animals," the Scribe said, startling Owen.

He patted one of the flyers on the head. "I just treat them better than the Dragon's guards ever did. A little kindness goes a long way."

"You are a strong leader," the Scribe continued, "able to reason with men. And there is a certain look in you that makes me wonder—"

"You should not jump to conclusions," Owen said.

"I've regained more than just my faculties," the Scribe said. "I remember now. And I can see him in you."

Owen turned. "Please, I don't want the people to know until the time is right. Certain of them have already rejected me once."

"They simply see you as a threat."

Owen shook his head. "Not just them. The book says, 'The King's Son is not welcome in his own land and not recognized. He has nowhere to lay his head.' When the time is right, it will be revealed to them."

"Then what do you want from me?"

"I have bad news," Owen said, gazing at the camp. "You have done much to make this your home. But you have to leave. All of you."

The Scribe looked horrified. "If I did not believe you were the one, I would call you mad."

"This mountain will be brought low—I'm hoping sooner rather than later."

"You hope this?"

"For the good of the people and the good of this land. Don't question me, for I must make a difficult journey and—"

"How can you leave us when the battle is about to commence?"

"I can't say I understand it all either. But this is what my father wishes. If you believe in me and want to help the people, convince them to go down from this mountain and prepare for war. If they stay here, I shudder to think what will happen."

"When must we go?"

"This morning if possible. Have them gather whatever

supplies they can carry. It is the only way to preserve this army and their safety."

Owen told him Mordecai and Erol and his clan should be coming to meet them soon. He gathered supplies, said good-bye to his new friends, got a hug and a kiss from Rachel, and returned to the transport flyers.

"Gentlemen, we have a Watcher to find," Owen whispered. "And a Mucker and a book."

The flyers seemed to jockey for position, each trying to go lower than the other so Owen would choose to ride on its back.

Dreyanna emerged from the cave and threw him some animal skins. "For your journey, Wormling. Return to us whole."

"Ah, half a Wormling is better than none, right?"

She shook her head. "Return whole."

"Keep an eye on your husband and that temper of his."

"That temper makes him who he is."

Owen nodded. "But a temper under control is more suitable for the army I desire."

Somewhere birds sang and animals skittered for the last of their food supply before the full force of winter bore down. Somewhere children laughed and played. Somewhere all was well.

But not here.

Here on the wet earth where trees bore barren branches and seemed to pray for sunshine, even the rocks cried out for something dry.

Here on this feather-strewn bog lay two figures, still and broken, appearing lifeless in repose. Onto this bleak scene strutted an animal—not a cute one with a pleasant face that you would want to take home. No, this was a brown and black jargid, its naturally smelly, repulsive fur matted from walking near the bog. Known for eating just about anything dead—fruit, mice, insects—it ambled toward the bodies in the mud.

The jargid's nose twitched as it sniffed the large bird with the curled claws and open eyes, reflecting the pale, cloudy sky. The jargid moved past the broken wing and sneezed as feathers tickled its nose. It shook its head and quickly moved on to the next creature—more bite-size. It had hooves and a body like some fast-running animal of the plains but a pointy face like a rat's. The jargid sniffed the soft underbelly, feeling the warmth inside. *Hmm. Couldn't have been here long.*

The jargid jumped back as something moved under the fur of the smaller beast. A worm! Nestled in a fresh kill?

Licking its lips, the jargid bared its teeth and leaned in for a taste of dead flesh. But the worm raised its head and bared teeth of its own! Tiny though they were, they sank into the jargid's lower lip, making him fall back and lick blood from his mouth. It seemed the little creature was taunting him now, but jargids are not creatures prone to effort, let alone confrontation, so he just shook his head and moved along, sniffing for something that had been dead much longer.

♦♦♦

The worm, however, moved up the fur of the dead-looking muddy animal, past the open lips and the bared teeth, up the soft, furry face, onto one ear, where there was very little hair on pure flesh. Mucker, with tenderness, sank his teeth into the ear.

Suddenly Watcher shook her head so hard that Mucker flew off and plopped into a puddle.

♦♦♦

Watcher stared at the gray clouds tinged with the pink of morning. She was wet and cold and so sore that she didn't even want to move a hoof. She noticed a jargid with a mouse in its mouth. Had the jargid bitten her, thinking she was dead?

She heard gurgling and lifted her head to find Mucker struggling in a small puddle. It wasn't deep, but water was the worm's worst enemy. She tried to stand, but pain shot down her back, and her yelp echoed over the bog. She stretched far enough to nose Mucker out of the puddle, then collapsed, every muscle and bone aching.

Mucker crawled onto Watcher's back and burrowed into her matted fur and made Watcher feel warm all over. To know she had a friend in this grim place gave her hope.

The big bird lay nearby, its left wing at a weird angle.

"Machree?" Watcher struggled to her feet, groaning and shaking, the pain almost too much to bear.

Machree's eyes were glazed over, and Watcher slumped,

recalling the screech of the demon flyer and the sickening crack of bones in the bird's back. She hung her head, remembering the falling, falling, falling and the wind in her ears. She did not remember impact, though it was clear the bird had taken the brunt of it.

"You misled me," a voice rasped.

"You're alive, Machree! Are you all right?"

"You told me you could sense invisibles," he said.

Watcher hung her head. "I always could before."

"Before what?"

"Watchers must pledge to always be truthful. Otherwise, we lose our power."

"And you were not truthful with me?"

"When I told you I trusted you more than Rotag and Tusin, I lied."

The bird tried to get up but mostly just flopped. Watcher tried to help, but she was too small.

"My wing is broken. I'll never fly again."

"Don't say that," Watcher said. "In time you will heal."

Machree gazed at the sky as a screech filled the air. "We will soon be demon flyer meat."

Owen felt safe on the back of the
transport flyer. He hunkered
down under the animal skin and set
a course for the cave where Watcher
and Humphrey should be waiting. He
didn't have to fear intervention by
demon flyers, because they wouldn't
attack their own.

Owen decided to refer to the larger,
older flyer as Grandpa and the slender
one with large eyes as Petunia. By
looking over Grandpa's shoulder, he
could see the ground, the interesting
rock formations, and the rolling plains
and forests.

He spotted a line of people moving slowly in single file, but when he

pushed Grandpa lower, the line scattered and several archers took their places.

"Erol!" Owen shouted. "Mordecai! It's me!"

He must have been traveling too fast and too high for them to hear, because the archers began to fire. He pulled up on Grandpa's neck, and they ascended out of reach of the arrows.

"Those are my friends," Owen said, looking over his shoulder. "They thought they were under attack. But at least the army is growing. We have a formidable force, and they're headed the right direction."

Grandpa and Petunia responded to a disturbance on the surface of a boggy creek, so Owen let them swoop toward it. They flew sideways, dipping in tandem, and Owen marveled at how agile they were for their size. If he could train them, they could become great assets.

When a mass of water and feathers shot into the air in a struggle that looked like war, the transport flyers angled straight toward the scene, then pulled up at the last moment and began to fly away.

"Help!" someone shouted.

Watcher!

Petunia kept her distance, hovering, but Grandpa allowed Owen to direct him back and plunged like a rock. Owen saw why the flyers had hesitated. From the flying feathers, Owen could tell invisible beings were tearing at the huge bird on the ground, and Watcher was trying to pull him away. The bird was trying to scoot away on a damaged wing, and already he appeared half shaved with blood oozing from his side.

"Attack!" Owen ordered.

Grandpa hesitated.

With teeth clenched and face forward, Owen hissed, "In the name of the King and for his kingdom, attack!"

Owen held tight as Grandpa's wings formed a V and he dived straight for the rustling feathers. He hit something solid and sent it crashing into the water. When something slashed at Grandpa's neck, he let out a cry and turned, hitting the invisible being with his tail. But another being grabbed Grandpa's leg and snarled, ripping into the flesh.

Owen leaped from the flyer's shoulders and fell onto the bird's feathers, rolling to a stop in the water.

"Wormling!" Watcher said. "They're ripping Machree to shreds! If only you had your sword!"

Owen looked to the sky. "Petunia! Attack!"

Now Grandpa and Petunia flew as one, locking wings and heading straight for the massive bird. The force of the wind knocked Owen and Watcher to the ground, and they heard a *kerthunk* as two bodies plopped into a muddy hole. In all their wriggling to escape, mud splattered their invisible bodies and they became visible to Owen.

They had the pointed heads of dragons but longer teeth

that looked just as sharp. Their bodies were sleek and lithe like a snake's, and their wings made them look more like rockets than flying beasts.

Grandpa and Petunia timed their next move perfectly. They let go of each other's wing and pirouetted so their tails slapped the demon flyers toward the trees, splintering the treetops.

Owen thought Watcher was running away, but she returned quickly with *The Book of the King*. "Read this to them!"

Owen had so missed Watcher's quick thinking. He read aloud:

> "Hear the words of the King! The King will make the flying beasts obey his Son, and no harm shall befall him. Neither will they hurt his friends when he commands, for they will be lifted up and cared for."

The demon flyers hissed at him, and like cornered cats that can do nothing but spit, they gnashed their teeth and cried, then rose in a flash and were gone.

Finally it was time for hugs and pats on the back and smiles and laughter for Owen and Watcher. There was so much to talk about, so much to tell, but Owen couldn't help but be concerned about the great bird that lay before him.

"You were coming for me, Watcher?" he said.

Watcher quickly told him the whole story of the Changeling and their friends from the castle. "I knew you would need the book and Mucker, but—" Her voice broke, and she dipped her head.

"But what, Watcher?"

The bird groaned.

"Nothing," Watcher said. "Let's get Machree some help."

Owen determined that the bird's wounds were grave.

"Are you really the Wormling she's been talking about?" the bird gasped.

Owen stroked the bird's head and nodded. "We're going to get you help before those flyers come back."

"Where?" Watcher whispered.

"If we leave him here, he'll sink and drown," Owen said.

"We certainly can't carry him."

The wind rose again, and Watcher ducked strangely, as if surprised by something from above.

Grandpa and Petunia took their places on either side of Machree, and with a mighty heave of their wings, they rolled the bird into position on Petunia's back.

Owen and Watcher climbed aboard Grandpa and followed.

Wings flapped and a sentry called out a warning, but the Dragon signaled to RHM that the two demon flyers were allowed into his lair, where he was meeting with his council. His red eyes burned in the darkness, watching these two shake with delight at the very thought of being in his presence. They would not have dared approach him without a message of importance, so he tolerated their mud-splattered bodies.

The flyers mince-stepped forward, heads down, wings back, paying homage. He growled at them to get on with it, and they finally looked up and walked forward, standing at attention.

"We've seen him," the first flyer said.

"Yes," the second chimed, "and that Watcher of his."

The first flyer looked around at the council members. "We attacked the great bird who had flown from his forest perch. It was dark when I threw it to the ground, and we thought it was dead."

"What great bird?" the Dragon said.

"Machree, Your Majesty," the second said. "In the morning we returned to finish the job, and that's when we saw the Watcher."

"You said you saw *him*," RHM said. "Who?"

"The Wormling, of course," the first flyer said. "We were about to feast on the carcass of the bird, removing the feathers first, when he swooped down on the back of a transport flyer."

"Transport?" the Dragon said, squinting.

RHM moved closer and lowered his voice. "There was a report of two transport—"

"Yes, I know," the Dragon hissed and turned back to the demon flyer. "Go on!"

"He attacked and chased us away."

"How do you know it was him?" the Dragon said. "Have you seen the Wormling before?"

"It was his words. He spoke with authority—"

"As if straight from his heart," the second flyer said. "Straight from the K—"

The first clamped a wing over the other's mouth.

The Dragon seethed. "Don't go sappy on me now!"

"He didn't know, sire."

The Dragon stood and paced. "Why didn't you capture him and bring him here?"

The flyers' eyes darted among the council. "Well," one said, "he seemed so authoritative and powerful, it was clear we had to get here as quickly as possible to inform you of his whereabouts."

"So do! Where is he?"

"Heading toward the line of people moving through the valley, Your Majesty. In the direction of the White Mountain."

The second held up a wing and dipped his head, like a child afraid of asking for a cookie. "One more thing, sire, if Your Majesty will allow me—"

"Just say it!"

"Right. Well, a strange thing happened. The Watcher never sensed us. Usually she sees us a long way off, but it was almost as if—"

"She has lost her powers."

"Exactly."

"Thank you. Dismissed."

RHM saw the two out, and members of the council began throwing ideas at the Dragon.

"Marshal the army and make sure this Wormling is dead," General Prufro said. He was a fat, scaly beast with giant incisors that made him whistle when he talked. "Descend on him while his Watcher is incapacitated."

"That was the job I gave Slugspike. But since he's failing miserably, I will do it myself. RHM, send me your most trusted demon flyer—"

"But, Your Majesty," the general said, "I firmly believe—"

A rattle formed in the Dragon's throat. Fighting to hold back the fire within, he snapped, "I know where he's going! And when he gets there, he will be more vulnerable than he can imagine. I will strike him down and cleanse this world."

The Dragon ordered that the refined gems be taken to the White Mountain.

"The supply is not complete," RHM said.

"Take what you have and move it into the mouth of the cave. And quickly."

Back in the Highlands—in Owen's world, where he lived above a used-book store and read to his heart's content—life continued despite his absence. As soon as he had left, darkness fell over the land like a blanket. Even people with normally happy dispositions walked with heads down or stayed inside behind closed blinds.

It is to this locale and away from the primitive life of the Lowlands that we return now to walk lighted streets on paved sidewalks. This is much like your world, with cars and planes and audio players and bullies in the hallway. It is a world vastly different from what Owen has experienced in the

Lowlands, yet it has many of the same concerns. But these people cannot see the fight going on around them.

Through the shadows of this world, on a street with few cars and only one business still open toward the end of that street, walks a young girl, a cape drawn over her shoulders and gathered about her head. She seems to know exactly where she is going, but sometimes she fearfully peers out of her cape to look behind her or across the street.

She passes under a streetlamp, and it suddenly flickers and flashes. She looks up, and just before the lamp goes dark, we are able to see her face—beautiful, soft and tender, and full of charm.

She continues down the street toward the tavern with its laughter and music and the smell of freshly baked potatoes and homemade bread and meat on a grill. She looks as if she could use a good meal, for her frame is slight and she appears no heavier than a butterfly.

She studies the glowing light of a fire flickering through the tavern window, listening to the clink of silverware and the calls for more bread or drink. Next door is a huge window and a door with a sign overhead: Tattered Treasures. The place looks abandoned, though books still line the shelves. No coats or hats on the rack beside the door. Yellow police tape strung across this door says Do Not Cross.

When a dark figure approaches from down the street, she

walks past the tavern and around the other side. From there she runs down the alley, displaying impressive speed, and turns the corner to find a man in a long, white apron scraping potato peels into a trash bin. He wipes his brow, covers the trash, and stands gazing at the back of the Tattered Treasures building next to the tavern. Finally the man hurries back inside.

The shrouded figure appears at the end of the alley, so the girl quickly jumps onto the Tattered Treasures fire escape. Climbing to the second story, she finds the window unlocked, dives in onto a squeaky bed, and fumbles in the dark to close the window. Below she sees the figure round the corner, scanning the alley. Trying to lock the window, she breaks off the ancient metal piece, and it clatters to the floor.

She ducks, holding her breath, unable to bring herself to look out again to see if he passes.

She scans the bookshelves in the moonlight, having become a great lover of books since meeting Owen. She notices three books on the floor and reaches to feel the leather spines. Were these his favorites or simply ones he had been reading before he left?

She feels awkward here, as if not only trespassing on a crime scene but also trespassing on Owen's life. She gingerly passes through the living room, past Mr. Reeder's room, and runs into the kitchen table, banging her thigh. On the table a newspaper headline reads "Search for Missing Boy Continues."

She can recite the story by heart. The local high school notified authorities that Owen was missing. His father gave the police no information and was taken in for questioning. Petrov, a worker at the tavern next door, told the reporter that Owen was a nice young man who didn't get into trouble and was obedient. Clara Secrest, a classmate, said Owen had trouble with some boys at the school. The bookstore closed, and bloodhounds found no trace of the boy.

The events of the past come flooding back to Constance— or Connie, as Owen called her. She had followed him instead of going to school one day, and that had set in motion events that brought them face-to-face with a beast so hideous and powerful that she shudders just thinking about it.

She walks down the stairs and wanders through the store, remembering the look on the face of Mr. Page, the old man who had given the strange book to Owen. It had been in the front room where he had cut Owen's foot and removed something from it. The man whispered to Constance—something that made her fearful and encouraged her at the same time. And then he simply disappeared.

A noise in the back room snaps her back to reality. She shrinks to the floor and crawls under the desk. A door opens and she holds her breath as the footsteps stop, then move toward her.

Two shoes, beaten and weathered, and the pants look like something a homeless person would wear. The floor creaks as the intruder walks toward the front desk. She gasps when he speaks.

"Where are you, little girl? And what are you doing here? Have you come looking for him?"

Her hands shake, and she feels an urge to go to the bathroom. A really bad urge. But she stays frozen under that desk, watching the feet move to the window facing the street. Then nothing. Has he left?

Connie listens carefully, barely able to hear anything over her pounding heart. What would Fern in *Charlotte's Web* do in this position? Or Nancy Drew?

When she can stand it no longer, she crawls forward and looks around the corner of the desk. She moves to the door. Still locked.

Her heart races again and she looks up, expecting to see him hovering.

Staying low, she runs to the bathroom, teeth chattering, mind wandering. She sits in the dark, then runs the water, gently washing her hands, careful not to make noise.

Back toward the front of the store she freezes at the sight of a man outside. But he isn't coming through the door—he's coming through the window. She prepares herself for the terrific crash of glass, but it never comes. The man has walked directly through the window!

Connie slips into the history section and kneels, hoping he hasn't seen her. When she hears the rattle of the back door, she wonders why he has used a door at all.

Finally she moves back into the fiction room and climbs the shelves, looking for the Medusa-head bookend she had seen Mr. Page pull. It wasn't there. Someone had smashed it on the floor. She climbs back down, examines the shelf, and tries to remember what Owen told her about the entrance.

If a Medusa head opened the shelf before, there must be something up there to do it again, she thinks.

Connie climbs up on the shelf, higher now, and shoves books aside, finally finding the place where the Medusa head had rested. A stone base remains, and in the middle there's a hole. She sticks her finger in but can't move the mechanism inside.

She climbs down again, getting tired of all the climbing, and runs to the front desk to grab a letter opener. When she jams it into the hole and pulls, the bookshelf moves and she slips behind it.

42

Pursued

The bookshelf closed behind Constance, and she plunged into total darkness. No torches this time. Carefully she made her way down, fearing the horrid creature she had glimpsed trying to catch them—Mr. Page had called it a Slimesees.

With her hand on the curving wall, she reached the last step, where she encountered a musty, salty smell she associated with the ocean. She moved to her right down a narrow corridor toward a pinpoint of flickering light. This was the way she and Owen had come with Mr. Page.

The light turned out to be a glowing torch, and Constance was determined to have it. She climbed the wall, wedging her feet between wet stones. It took all her strength to balance herself while pulling the torch from its holder.

No sooner was she on the ground than she heard rustling behind her. She quickly moved away, retracing steps she and Owen had taken so long ago.

Through passage after passage, trying one underground channel, then another, backing up and trying again, Constance tried to recall the route they had taken. When with Mr. Page and Owen, she had simply followed and hadn't paid much attention.

Strangely, despite her fear and the danger, Constance's mind raced with how much her life had changed since Owen's departure. Her mother no longer went to the bookstore to clean. Constance went to school and faithfully did her home-work, but she was just going through the motions, simply biding time. For what, she didn't know. But with every step toward school, home, or the library (the only other place she was allowed), she sensed someone following her. And when she had been frightened by a wing flap overhead, she told her mother.

"Nonsense," the woman said, but her look betrayed her.

Constance had to wonder if some kind of presence had also triggered a fear in her mother.

"Yes, Mother," Constance had said. She had retreated to

her room, turned out her light, and looked out the window, waiting for watching eyes. It was those eyes she had been afraid to alert when she had slipped out, down the back stairs and into the alley, while her mother was sleeping. Cloaked and walking in shadows, she had gone unnoticed in her corner of the world and had walked the familiar streets to the bookstore.

She had passed the Briarwood Café and stared through the window at the girl with the long, flowing hair who wiped the countertop with a rag. This was the girl Owen had taken to the movies, and Constance wished she could be as beautiful as Clara.

Constance had a friend who said she could tell the future. "I think you'll get married," her friend had said. "And he'll be some congressman or governor or maybe even the president. Yes, the president of the whole country. You'll live in a big house, and people will wait on you. They'll take pictures of you getting in and out of your car and stuff like that."

Constance had laughed, because she knew no one could tell the future—especially her friend. Still, the idea intrigued her. With all she had suffered, could her grown-up life be destined for something grand?

Constance came to a bend in the tunnel where she, Owen, and Mr. Page had rested and talked after the winged beast had attacked them in the old bed-and-breakfast place—the B and

B. Something had drawn them there to meet that man, and now she felt as if she was being drawn again. But why? What secrets did this underground tunnel and the B and B hold?

The beast that had chased them had shot fire down a shaft, and as Constance drew close to it, she saw the charred wood along the floor where the flames had licked. The sight sent shivers through her, recalling the overwhelming fear, but Mr. Page's calm had soothed her and infused her with a resolve to survive.

But now dread surfaced as a blast of air shot through the tunnel, making the torch flutter and nearly go out. A sound filled the room, a humming, buzzing, whine of a small motor or perhaps of a large animal.

The bottom of the elevator shaft remained intact, though the top and sides had been charred. The rustling behind her seemed closer now. She threw the torch toward the opening and backed into the enclosure, peeking through the wood slats of the cage. Mr. Page had lowered them with a pulley and crank, so Constance grabbed for the hanging chain. Could this damaged contraption possibly still hold her?

Someone moved past the torch, and shadows danced on the wall.

Constance pulled the chain with all her might, and it was then that she realized the humming was coming from above.

She gave another tug, straining with every ounce of strength, and the elevator began to ascend.

Something small flew past her and she swatted at it, but the chain began to slip from her other hand. She grabbed with both hands again, and something buzzed near her ear. But she had to keep pulling. The floor began to crack. Just as she feared she would fall through, an arm grabbed her from below.

Constance screamed as she flew out of the cage, and it crashed to the ground.

Owen could tell Erol and Mordecai were happy to see him and Watcher, though he had to convince them not to shoot at the transport flyer. When they had moved to a safe place in a wooded area with the clan and those they had enlisted (quite a throng), Petunia landed with Machree. Several of the women tended to the huge bird.

"More warriors are coming from the mountain," Owen said. "My friend Connor is leading them, and the Scribe and Burden are with them."

Mordecai said, "Then we will wage war soon."

"Not until I return from a final journey to the Highlands," Owen said.

"What for?" Mordecai said. "We need you here. *The Book of the King* says the Son shall—"

"We will follow the book to the letter," Owen said, glancing at Watcher. "But I must go to the Highlands."

A screech in the sky made them look up to see that Petunia and Grandpa had taken flight again. They dipped their wings and shrank into the shadows underneath trees.

"Don't worry about them," Owen said. "These two are loyal to the King now."

Erol shuddered. "It's not them I'm worried about. The demon flyers are on the move. They're heading north toward the mountain."

"Why didn't you warn us?" Owen asked Watcher.

She lowered her head. "I didn't sense it."

Owen stared at her, wondering what had happened. Instead of confronting her, he said, "I must hurry. Be on your guard. Under no circumstances should you go to battle without me."

"You want to be here to see the slaughter?" Mordecai said, smiling.

"I want to be here to celebrate the victory for the King."

He ran for Grandpa, and Watcher followed. The beast seemed reluctant to come out from the safety of the trees. "You have nothing to fear from me," Owen said.

"He fears what is in the air," Watcher said.

"As well he should, but as the book says, 'Those who live for the King shall cast out fear and live free from it. It no longer has dominion over us when we follow him.'"

"Let me go with you as far as the White Mountain. I can bring the transport flyer back here."

It was too dangerous, and Owen needed her here. But the look in her eyes let him know it was no use to say no.

They flew on the back of Grandpa, low to the trees and with clouds blocking them from the view of the demon flyers.

"They're delivering gemstones," Owen said. "It's part of the Dragon's plan, which makes it even more important for us to hurry."

Below them marched the warriors from Yodom.

"Watcher!" Owen called out. "Land near them on the way back and tell them where to meet Erol and Mordecai's group!"

Farther up the mountain and through the pass it became much colder, and Grandpa had a hard time staying aloft. Watcher wasn't talking and seemed distant.

Owen had Grandpa land and said he would go the rest of the way on foot. "Watcher, return for Humphrey," he said. "And do everything you can to help expand the army, but make sure Connor doesn't take things into his own hands before I return." He paused. "Is there something on your mind?"

Watcher's big eyes glistened and her lower lip twitched. "I can't help you anymore," she said, sobbing. "My powers are gone. I have betrayed you, my people, and worst of all, the King himself."

Owen lifted her head. "What happened?"

Watcher closed her eyes and bowed her head. "I lied to Machree to get him to help, and that has made all the difference."

Owen knelt before her and hugged her neck. "Watcher, I could never have a greater friend. I wouldn't even be alive if not for you."

"But I have let you down, right when you needed me most."

Owen pursed his lips. "If only I had my sword."

"Your sword could not undo my wrong, could not bring back my powers. I might as well surrender to the Dragon now."

"Don't say that. You know *The Book of the King* states, 'When the Son comes, he will make everything new again. The old will pass away, and the original order will be restored.'"

"But what does that mean for me? I'm of no use."

"Your powers have protected us," Owen said. "But it is who you are that is most important. Your true heart of repentance pleases me most and the King."

"I'll never see the Son," she said. "He would not want to know such a one as me."

Owen smiled. "I assure you, friend, he wants to see you very much."

"Have you found him?" she said, gasping.

"Many things I have not been able to tell you, things I have discovered. I will explain when I return."

"With the Son?"

Owen paused. "When I return, you will see the Son."

A screech from above sent shivers through Watcher's body, and Owen loosed her. "I must go." He took Mucker from her back and tucked him inside his shirt. "Do not despair. You will be forgiven and your powers restored. Trust me."

44

The Release

Constance struggled against the man who pulled her from the elevator, her feet barely touching the ground. "Let me go!"

"You don't understand," the man said, his voice scratchy and cold. "You have released the minions before their time."

"I what?" she said.

When they reached the turn, the man bent to pick up the torch, and the flame illuminated his face. An eye drooped, and scars ran from his head down his face and neck, leaving a hideous mess of fire-ravaged skin and bone. Wisps of hair were threaded over an otherwise bare, shiny skull.

Constance couldn't even breathe, let alone cry out. Why had she slipped out of her home and come to the bookstore?

The man held the torch close and looked her over. "Have you been stung?"

Her mouth moved, but she couldn't utter a sound.

"Did they bite you?"

She shook her head.

"What were you looking for down here?" the man said.

She looked back at the elevator cage, in pieces on the ground. He pulled her through the opening and back into the channel.

"I was in the bookstore," she managed, "and someone came in. I merely wanted to get away."

"Why were you there?" the man said, his voice like gravel.

"Looking for a friend," Constance said. "You wouldn't know him."

The yellow flame dancing beside him cast an eerie glow but allowed Constance to look past the shocking face and see into his eyes. They were set deep and dark, but they had the look of knowledge and wisdom—and love.

"You're him," she said, "aren't you? The man who—"

A noise startled her, and they both turned. A scream and buzz filled the air, and off came the man's coat. He threw it over her. "On the ground! Quickly!"

Shrouded, Constance could only imagine what was happening. The torch whooshed, and she pictured the man swinging it like a baseball bat, fending off whatever was attacking. Bees? Some sort of creature that lived only in this underworld?

The man grunted and struggled, and Constance lifted the coat enough to peek. The winged creatures easily evaded the torch and swarmed him, then moved away.

One was finally knocked to the ground by a mighty swing, and in the sparkling light Constance examined it. The wings were thick like leather and ribbed like a snake's back. It had a series of short legs underneath with sticky spines protruding, and when it finally righted itself and stood, it looked directly at Constance. The pupils grew smaller, and it opened its mouth in a scream or a call.

Constance screamed at its protruding jagged teeth—the incisors much longer with something black dripping from them. Its tiny, forked tongue snaked out between the lower teeth. It darted underneath the coat before she could slam it onto the floor.

Then the rest of the hissing and flapping creatures swarmed her.

"Are you all right?" the man yelled.

"I think one of them flew under here with me."

"Don't move." He wrapped the coat around her and picked her up, running like a much younger man. After a few turns, the man lifted the coat from her face and held the torch close, his eyes filled with alarm.

She turned to see on her shoulder a winged creature, baring its fangs before sinking its teeth into her skin.

45

The Task

Owen found the passage where he had led Connor and the others out of the White Mountain. When he and Mucker reached the end, Owen scraped away some of the dirt. "See, it's not rock, just dirt from the explosion. Can you get us inside?"

Mucker pulled back, as if to say, "Hey, it's me you're talking to."

"The explosion sealed the Dragon's workers inside, but he'll be back. He wants to destroy this world—I've read it in the book."

Mucker's face grew grave, and he lifted his eyes as if to say, "What are we waiting for?"

Owen pulled out *The Book of the King* and turned to a passage from the section called Triumph.

> "Happy are those who help the weak. The King will deliver them in times of distress.
>
> The King cares for and preserves his faithful ones. He will help them enter into the promise he has given.
>
> When your enemy lies in wait, when he is ready to devour, and when he gathers his forces to slay the chosen one, do not be afraid, for greater is the King than any enemy or any insult he can muster.
>
> Rejoice and be glad and wait for the deliverance of the King."

Owen was so engrossed in the words of the book that he was surprised to look up and see how big Mucker had become, chewing through the passage with abandon. The air became tinged with an acrid smell, and Owen felt liquid running across Mucker's back and sides.

When Mucker finally broke through to the other side, Owen found the bodies of two who had followed them into the tunnels. The explosion he and Connor had rigged here had sealed the escape, but Owen was surprised to see most of the rooms where his friends had toiled were still intact.

Owen instructed Mucker to rechannel the liquid into the tunnel he had dug so it could seep through the loose earth.

When Mucker was done, there was not a trace of the flammable liquid, save in the Great Hall.

Remembering what had happened here filled Owen with thanksgiving. Had he never come here, he wouldn't have known where to find the portal to the Highlands, wouldn't have been able to save Connor and the others, and wouldn't have discovered the meaning of the prophecy:

> Before the Great War shall come a time that shall seem like the end, for the Wormling will be consumed with fire from above and the enemy will rule for a short time in the Lowlands. Do not fear when the White Mountain is laid low, for this will not be the end. It will signal only the coming of the Son, the rightful heir to the throne.

Owen led Mucker into the Great Hall, where he had faced the neodim. "There's something here I must show you," Owen said. "And we must be quick about our task."

The Dragon flew like a missile with RHM by his side. He didn't care that all the gemstones were not in place, that this outsider had thwarted his plan, or that when he came upon the scene it was likely his ultimate hope would not be accomplished. All he cared about now was that he would be rid of this pesky outsider who stuck in his craw like a bone in his throat.

"Are you sure he is there?" the Dragon hissed as he soared.

"Demon flyers report seeing him fly in on one of the transport flyers, and that Watcher of his was with him as well."

"Unable to sense like she used to."

The Dragon laughed, a rattle in his throat. It was always like this just before an attack. He coughed and sputtered and drew juices from within, amassing an enormous amount so that when he struck, molten fire would melt his enemies where they stood.

The Dragon pressed on, gaining speed, tightening his talons on something beneath him, something not even RHM knew he held. The surprise to his victim would be doubled when the silver sword hurtled down at him along with the belch of fire.

A demon flyer approached and fell into formation with them. "All the stones are there, Your Majesty. At least all we've gathered."

"Good," the Dragon said. "Leave the gems at the entrance, where they will do the most damage."

"How is that, Your Highness?"

The Dragon rolled his eyes. How could he explain the magic of the stones or that he had gleaned this from *The Book of the King* itself? The destruction of the Lowlands would come from the gems and the fire and the leveling of the mountain. "Be gone and prepare your followers for an assault on the forces of the Wormling. Those not killed by the blast shall be killed the conventional way."

The demon flyer left, and before them rose the white-capped mountain. The Dragon descended below the clouds and tested his fire on treetops with a simple snort. He was in fine fire indeed.

But he was no farther than the approach to the putrid town of Yodom when a demon flyer came out of nowhere, screeching. "He's there, sire! We saw him at the entrance to the mountain high above! He's mocking you, saying you are not powerful enough to destroy him."

The eyes of the Dragon turned crimson, and he shot into the air at earsplitting speed. Above the clouds, the Sword of the Wormling glistened silver and gold.

"Stay back!" the Dragon called to RHM and the demon flyers. "The Wormling is mine!"

47

Words and Fire

When Owen had first come to the White Mountain, he had seen a dead man frozen in the ice below the mouth of the cave that led into the belly of even more pain and struggle and death. He had found workers so fatigued they could barely walk. The mountain was a beauty from a distance, but up close it proved the downfall of many, and that is exactly why Owen had come here. This place would signal the death of the Wormling. Forever.

Owen made his way through the webs and over the gemstones at the mouth of the mountain. These stones could actually help, he thought, as he hollered insults he knew the demon flyers would hear. When the sky began to cloud and darkness covered the setting sun and the orange and gold on the horizon, Owen knew the old Dragon was on his way to see not just the end of him but also the end of the whole plan of the King.

But there were things the Dragon did not know—could not know—from *The Book of the King*, no matter how much he had read. The book speaks to the pure in heart and reveals to those dedicated to the Sovereign things normal readers cannot understand, certainly not those whose hearts are as prickly and stony as the Dragon's.

Owen took a deep breath and yelled, "There is a reason the Dragon is usually alone in his lair and must call for a meeting of his council if he wants company: no one can stand the smell of him! He is a pimple on the face of this world, and the King will expunge him from it one day!"

The last thing Owen wanted was for the Dragon to see the liquid cascading out of the mountain from the back side or for the Dragon to enter through the soft earth Mucker had overturned. The demon flyers screeched and retreated, but it wasn't until he saw the smoky trail below and heard the echoes of wing flaps that he knew his plan had worked.

He stood on a pile of gemstones and shouted to the heavens, "There is no King but the true King! Though mountains may rise and fall, though foes come against him, he will be exalted above every living thing. Let the rocks cry out. Let the trees tell of his glory!"

This speech, of course, was meant not just to strengthen Owen's heart or displease the Dragon but also as a signal to a friend below.

Clouds roiled and rose like smoke from a furnace.

"Now, let the evil one be thrown down! Though he makes his bed in the depths of the ocean or on the top of the highest mountain, he can never escape the awful day of the King!"

As the white clouds churned, Owen watched, mesmerized by the Dragon's rise. A small voice inside him—his own or Watcher's?—told him it was time, but he lingered.

"Those who oppose the King," he was whispering now, "shall see their end come quickly."

Owen moved too close to the edge and knocked a gem-stone loose, sending it ticking its way down the pile, skittering right and left until it reached the hardened snow. It rolled and bounced into the thin air, and just as it was engulfed in the boiling clouds that inched ever closer, a pair of red eyes appeared and a mouth held the gemstone between razor-sharp teeth.

Owen's heart seemed to stop for a second as the Dragon spit out the stone and belched fire that melted the snow near the mouth of the cave.

Owen dived back over the pile of stones and slid through

the opening just as the fire engulfed the cave's mouth. The tunnel warmed so much that the webs melted and Owen slipped through unstopped. However, his plan that the Dragon be slowed by the gems was dashed when the huge beast burst into the cave and sent a wave of stones cascading.

Surely the narrow walls of the tunnel would slow him. Not even the neodim could get through many of these. However, the Dragon simply expanded his body so that the walls exploded around him.

"It is the King's pleasure to use the weak things of the world to amaze the strong!" Owen shouted as he slipped and slid down the tunnel, propelled by the surge of rocks and dirt. He came to a bend and a smaller opening ahead that he had crafted with Mucker—a shortcut that dropped straight to the Great Hall. Owen yelled into the darkness, "The King chose the insignificant and those considered nothing so he could dethrone those who think they are something!"

These words were not for the Dragon but for Mucker, but that did not stop the Dragon from responding. A yellow-orange streak belched from his hideous mouth and lit the tunnel like fireworks.

This cyclone of fire engulfed the tunnel, and as it reached Owen, he put his hands over his head and jumped into the smaller opening. He swirled down with the Dragon's pungent fire behind him.

48

Confrontation

Seething and resolved to tear the Wormling limb from limb, the Dragon plunged into the mountain like a ravenous cat that had a mouse by the tail. All his years of striving against the King had led to this moment. He had made promises, signed treaties, negotiated peace, all with one goal in mind: possessing this world, destroying it, and remaking it in his own image. That the Wormling was now taunting him with words of the King only made his anger boil more.

The pressure in these narrow passages was great, and he scratched and clawed deep into the earth with his talons to propel himself, moving earth and stone. He crashed with the stony crown of his head, butting and ramming himself deeper into the chasm. When he slowed at a narrow point, he took a breath and puffed his body out, breaking through to another level.

As he plunged, he expected to find neodim bodies. It was reported that the Wormling (with help from the rabble prisoners) had killed several. How they had done this the Dragon didn't know and didn't care. The death of weak followers was welcomed. It meant that only the strongest would survive. As for the others, he was glad to see them go.

He snorted fire into the darkness and searched for the Wormling, sniffing the air. He found a small entrance, a hole that looked like it had been recently dug, and stuck his nose inside. Smelling the creature, he gave another blast of fire.

Convinced he would not fit inside that small opening, he continued down the larger tunnel, breaking walls and smashing and thrashing until he burst through and stopped near the ledge overlooking the Great Hall. Rock and dirt cascaded, and the Dragon finally saw the decaying bodies of his neodim. He growled in disgust at the Wormling defiantly standing against the far wall of the hall below.

The Dragon stretched. "Who killed these?"

"Probably something they ate," the Wormling said. "Or perhaps they drowned under so much of your kindness."

"Insolent tramp!" the Dragon muttered. *Speaking as if he has authority.* "Who helped you?"

"I needed no help killing these. They had no real power. True power comes only from the King, and not even you have that kind of power."

The Dragon's throat rattled, and he spread his wings to lift a talon. It was not in his nature to keep his cool when angered, but the Dragon gritted his teeth and cocked his head at the small creature below him. "I have something for you, Wormling. Come out into the open where I can see you."

"What could you possibly have that would interest me?"

Metal clanged and the Wormling looked up.

"Recognize this?" the Dragon growled.

"I recognize it as well as you do," the Wormling said, "judging from that scar on your leg I gave you at the castle."

The Dragon spread his wings and lifted from the ledge, flying above the Wormling and swinging the sword back and forth, measuring the distance he would need to throw it and considering whether he should bring the Wormling to his knees and have him beg for his miserable life before it ended.

"Ironic, don't you think?" the Dragon said. "Slain by the very sword you were given to kill me."

"You've planned well," the Wormling said. "Because if you were to spit fire at me down here—"

"I don't spit fire!"

"—you would kill not only me but also yourself while blowing this whole mountain to the sky."

The Dragon hovered midflight. He hadn't considered this possibility, but he tried hard not to show it to the Wormling.

"With all the fuel you've gathered and with all that's pooled since the captives were freed, you'd be committing suicide to use fire here. Even more ironic, no? The fire-breathing Dragon killed by the very fire that he spits. Are you willing to sacrifice yourself for the good of your followers?"

The Dragon formulated a new plan on the spot, pleased with himself for thinking it through so quickly.

"Sword!" the Wormling shouted.

The hilt of the sword grew hot in the Dragon's talons, and he released it, then reached to get it back, but it was gone, hurtling through the air toward the Wormling. It appeared the Wormling would be impaled, but just as it reached him, the sharp tip flipped and the handle slapped into the Wormling's hand.

The Dragon plunged down, body shaking.

"Ah-ah-ah, I wouldn't do that," the Wormling said. "Dragon go boom if you go spit spit."

The Dragon sneered. "I promise you, you will be charred beyond recognition."

The Wormling put the sword at his side. "The King uses you, though you do not understand it. And I promise you,

Dragon, with everything that is within me, you will feel not just the tip of my sword but the entire blade up to the hilt buried deep into your heart."

The Dragon's eyes narrowed. "This is where you die, Wormling. And the world will be reborn."

Watcher flew back toward the others on the transport flyer. She had lost her powers, lost her ability to help the Wormling, and still he had accepted her. He valued her for simply being herself. That lightened her heart and at the same time puzzled her. How could this be?

Watcher landed ahead of the warriors coming from Yodom and managed to alert the archers of her identity before they shot her. The Scribe came out from the crowd in a long, flowing robe. His face had become even healthier with the exercise, and he seemed a different person from the scattered man who had lived in a tree.

Watcher told him about the clan of Erol awaiting them not far ahead and that Mordecai was with them. "And the Wormling went inside the White Mountain to—"

The ground trembled, and an explosion rocked the countryside.

"Look!" someone shouted. "The mountain!"

The top of the mountain was suddenly simply gone, and an avalanche cascaded.

A large beast flew above the mountain, wings spread wide.

"The Dragon," the Scribe gasped.

The beast paused as if gathering energy and spewed fire into the newly opened mountain. The inferno was like nothing Watcher had ever seen, and the Dragon toppled backward in the sky as ash and smoke billowed.

The Dragon regained his position, flapping wildly, watching the conflagration with glee. As if his mission was accomplished, he plunged from the mountain and flew about, roaring and bellowing.

The Scribe put a hand on Watcher's back. "Perhaps he didn't go inside the mountain. Perhaps he—"

"No," Watcher said, unable to move. "I saw him. And he could never survive an explosion like that."

50

Poisoned

Constance opened her eyes but couldn't keep them open. As her eyelids fluttered she was able to make out a dim room with two candles burning on a mantel. A wooden table and two chairs. A loaf of bread. Dusty curtains drawn over a window.

Her head felt like it was twice its normal size and throbbing, her nose running, and her throat scratchy and raw. Achy and feverish, her body was so chilled her teeth rattled. She wished this were the flu, but she knew better.

A chair creaked in the corner, and the man with the burned face sat forward in the dim light. Constance tried to sit up but could barely lift her head from the pillow.

"How do you feel?" The man's voice was deep and comforting.

"Nearly dead," she said. "It would be less painful to sleep and never wake up." The man brought her a glass of water, but her throat hurt so much she choked on it. "Where am I?"

"My cottage, a good distance from town. You're safe."

"What were those things? Bees?"

"Minions from the Dragon," the man said, staying in the shadows.

"The beast that chased us a long time ago in that old house?"

The man nodded.

"And what are minions?"

"They do the bidding of the evil one." He drew closer, and Constance could see the scars on his face and neck.

When she looked away, he brought a wooden bowl of strong-smelling salve and dabbed it on her shoulder. Constance lay back on the pillow.

"This will help draw the poison out. The minions accelerate the life cycle. I'm hoping the one that stung you hadn't reached full venom yet."

"What do you mean? They speed up life?"

The man lifted one of her hands so she could see it.

Constance gasped. It looked wrinkled and spotty like her mother's.

"The venom ages you too soon."

"Were you stung too," she said, "trying to fight them off?"

"I am immune." He gently let down her hand. "Now you must rest. Things will be better after you sleep longer."

"You say that as if you do not believe it."

"I believe it, but you may not feel the same when the venom takes full effect."

"What about my mother?" Constance asked. "What will she think when I don't come home?"

The man winced and looked away.

"What? Has something happened to her?"

"It is best if you rest. If I were to tell you the truth—"

"You challenged me with truth before Owen left us. Don't you remember that night and the things you said?"

"I do, but in your weakened state I don't know how much you can handle."

"Tell me about my mother."

The man lowered his head. "The woman you know as your mother is really just your caretaker. She is not of your blood."

"Impossible!" Constance said. "How could she not be my mother?"

"Things are not always as they seem, child."

"If she is not my mother, who is? Is she still alive?"

"I believe she is. And you will see her again in time."

"I don't dare even leave here with those minions about. Is there a way we can kill them?"

The man looked pained. "I'm afraid they've already been loosed. And the effect on the Highlands will be devastating."

"The Highlands?"

"Your world," the man said. "We call this the Highlands and the world Owen traveled to the Lowlands."

Constance closed her eyes. "I've been waiting a long time for him. Will he return?"

"Much has happened to him, I'm sure, but yes, he will return. Soon. Now rest."

51

Nicodemus

In the next room, standing in shadows, this man who was accustomed to regal raiment and having his every need cared for stood alone in nothing more than rags. His home could be called Spartan—another way of saying he had become poor and had very few worldly goods. The long coat that had been his trademark since coming to this small town was gone—burned in some horrible accident.

With hands clasped behind him and sensing that the visitor he had requested was now in the room, he spoke. "Nicodemus, it has been a long journey for you."

"And there is a longer road ahead, my King."

"How is he? Does he have the book again?"

"The good news is that he retrieved it, sire, and he had it with him as he entered the White Mountain. The bad news is that the Dragon followed him and—"

The man turned on Nicodemus and looked at him with great compassion. "You fear for his life?"

"O King, he has given of himself in so many ways. I have watched him come to know and love the people and creatures of the Lowlands. In every way he proves himself worthy to be called your Son."

"And yet?"

"And yet I fear he may have given the last full measure in hopes of protecting his companions."

The King fell silent a moment. Then, "And what of the Watcher?"

"She has lost her powers because of an indiscretion, but she is not hurt physically. Mordecai is now with the other warriors."

"Mordecai," the man whispered. He had taken Mordecai in when he was young and eventually charged him with protecting his family. "I always hoped he would return to me. My Son has made that hope a reality."

"Not only him, sire, but also the Scribe. His mind has returned, and he thinks clearly because of your words."

"What do you think happened to my Son?"

"The Dragon went inside and was seen a while later destroying the top of the mountain. There was fire, an explosion, and the mountain spewed the gemstones the Dragon has been mining with the help of the people he has imprisoned. Your wife included."

The King was heartbroken.

"Sire, there is no way he could have survived. The explosion blew the top off the mountain."

"Was anyone in the countryside killed?"

"Not that we know of, but it is enough that your Son was a casualty."

"Have you forgotten the prophecy?"

Nicodemus looked at the floor. "I trust in your insight and your will, O King. Who am I to question you?"

"You questioned whether you should stay with him or follow my orders and let him go alone."

"An indiscretion of my own, I'm afraid," Nicodemus said. "It was not because I don't trust you but because I distrust the Dragon."

The King's heart ached. "How are they to believe who cannot even read the prophecy or who have not heard my words? If you, who have seen me face-to-face and talked with me, cannot believe, how will they?"

"I do believe you, O King." Nicodemus fell to his knees. "And I trust you with my life and with his."

The man known as Mr. Page, who we now know is the King, put his hands on Nicodemus's shoulders. "Happy are those who have not seen me and still believe what I have said. They shall be set free by knowing the truth and shall be partakers of the wholeness the world will soon see."

52

Not Growing
Weary

Perhaps, like Nicodemus, you have lost hope for our hero, the one we said you would love from the moment you met him. His genuine heart and depth of courage overcome the fact that few of his friends know these deep qualities. Actually, only one of his friends in the Highlands truly understands the depths of his goodness, and even she does not yet truly comprehend the love of which he is capable.

But she will in time. A short time.

To assuage our fears about Owen, we must travel deep inside the earth and follow the chomping and munching of Mucker. Owen's eyes droop, and his head nods as he is swept along by his friend. Owen has been reading *The Book of the King* nonstop, devouring it, finding new and deeper meanings with each page, and his furious pace helps speed Mucker along.

> "Though the fire threatens to engulf, you will escape by the words of the Sovereign. Though the enemy seeks to take your life, trust in the King, and he will deliver you."

Owen had known the Dragon would have to get far enough away from the blast zone to keep himself from being killed, and it was in those moments of the beast's ascension that Owen rejoined Mucker in the tunnel and recited several passages one right after another. He had tried to drain all the liquid from the deep caverns but hoped the residual fuel would give the appearance that the Dragon's plan had worked. There would be a hole in the top of the mountain that would appease the Dragon, and, Owen prayed, no one in the surrounding area would be killed.

Mucker slowed when Owen quit reading, so he opened the book again.

> "The King gives strength to the weary and increases the power of the weak. Even young people grow tired, slip, and fall, but any who put their trust in the King will find new power. They will fly on winged creatures. They will

move through the night and not be tired. They will not grow faint, though the task ahead is arduous."

Owen patted Mucker's back. "These words are for us, my friend. Let us not grow weary. We will not stop until we are back in the Highlands."

The Dragon paced in his lair, snorting and scratching the underside of his leg. The scar there bothered him now more than ever.

Even with his armies encamped around the castle and fires burning brightly, something gnawed at him. He should have been elated over the death of the Wormling, dancing in his spacious ballroom, spreading a feast to end all feasts. All that was left was to find another way to destroy the worlds.

RHM knocked and entered timidly, head down.

"Bad news?" the Dragon said. "Or did my inspectors discover his bones?"

"Nothing, sire. Not the sword, not

the book or remnants thereof, or even charred bones. My guess is that you vaporized the creature."

"There would have been something of him down there," the Dragon spat. "And why, with all the fuel in the depths of that cavern, was the entire mountain not leveled? Why didn't the explosion send those gemstones throughout the entire kingdom?"

A commotion in the hallway drew RHM, who then led a demon flyer inside to see the Dragon.

"News from the Highlands, sire," the flyer said, gasping as if he had just flown all the way from there. "The girl who was being watched has disappeared. We heard from a sentinel that someone was inside the bookstore—where the Wormling had been kept."

"Inside? Who?"

"We're not sure, but it could have been the girl. Someone disturbed the minions, and some were loosed prematurely."

"Not all?"

"No, sire. The others are nearly ready."

The Dragon turned to RHM. "Do you see why I am skeptical?"

"Begging your pardon, sire," the demon flyer said, "but this was found in the tunnel near the minions' nest."

The creature handed the Dragon a piece of charred cloth.

The Dragon sniffed it and let out a roar. "It can't be him! He is dead!"

RHM and the flyer shrank back, but the Dragon merely walked to the window and gazed out at his troops. "If there must be war, let it begin before they even suspect it. Ready my troops. We will wipe out the enemy's army before it ever assembles."

Owen could tell they were close to the surface of the Highlands because the earth was darker and more fertile—good for farming. Mucker accelerated because Owen was so captivated by the book.

> "When the Son has been discovered and the portal is breached, prepare for wails and mourning. What is young shall become old, and that which is alive and vibrant shall be laid waste."

Owen pondered the words, falling silent long enough for Mucker to actually stop—not a good thing in the middle of the earth with no air pockets other than those provided by the hard-charging worm. Owen quickly realized this meant his own demise and began reading again.

> "But do not despair, for this has been written that you might know that victory is yours. The Son shall over-come the plan of the evil one through the strength of the King. And justice shall be given for the anguish and pain meted out by this enemy. Truly, a new chapter shall be written in the battle for the two worlds."

Owen was the Son, the one who would lead the army into battle. And he was the one who would marry the princess— a prospect almost more difficult to comprehend than winning a great battle. But if the King had prepared him for the fight, surely he would prepare him for a wedding and married life as well.

> "The Son shall find his bride perfectly suited for him—a friend and constant companion, one whose love cannot be compared."

That last made Owen blush. He didn't know a thing about girls, how to talk to them without stuttering and laughing. The closest he had come to normal conversation was with Clara Secrest back home, but how would he do with someone he didn't even know? If he could believe *The Book of the King* about being a warrior and the true Son, he could believe he would be given what he needed when it came time to face this love hurdle—the taking of a bride.

Mucker's munching and crunching accelerated, and soon he was through the loamy soil and into a small chamber just below the surface. Mucker took up nearly all the space in the chamber, and Owen moved around examining the scorched walls and a bare place in the middle of the earthen floor that hadn't been scorched at all. Owen stood in the middle of that bare spot and held his sword high. It clanked against something metal, and with a little probing, he cleared dirt and grass roots away to uncover a small circular door, like a manhole cover, with hinges and a spring.

The effort caused Owen to move the dirt at his feet and unearth a small metal object black as soot. He rolled it with his toe to where he could pick it up, and when he held it close, it seemed familiar.

He gasped. It was the object Mr. Page had removed from his heel so long ago! He put it in his pocket.

"What is this place, Mucker?" Owen said, noticing the worm had already begun to shrink.

Owen touched his sword to a small lever beside the spring, and the cover fell open into the hole. A shaft of sunlight hit him full in the face, and he had to shade his eyes.

Owen climbed through the hole to find the knoll burned

black. He sat staring at the town in the distance, glad to be home but also already longing for the Lowlands and his friends there.

A scream wafted over the hills and startled him. He hopped back inside the chamber and picked up Mucker, now about the size of a small dog, and tucked him under his arm. Shoving his sword through his belt, he climbed out and ran toward the town.

A faint buzzing met him near the almost deserted streets. A few cars passed, and a man coming out of a grocery store gave him a strange look, then opened his cell phone and made a call.

Owen headed for Tattered Treasures. He wasn't sure what he would say to the man who had pretended to be his father, but he wanted to hear his story.

He was near the laundry when a squad car pulled up, lights flashing. Two officers emerged and one said, "Hold it right there, son."

Owen stuck Mucker inside his shirt, and both officers pulled their guns. Owen realized they were focused on his sword.

"Hands in the air and turn around," the first officer said.

The second circled behind him and pulled the sword from his belt, whistling. "Sharp! No kid's toy. Where'd you get this?"

"From a friend."

"Been using it to dig? There's dirt on the edges. What were you planning to do with this?"

"Nothing. I was just walking home."

"Which is where?"

"The bookstore down the street."

The sword clanged against the concrete behind him. "What's your name, kid?"

"Owen. Owen Reeder."

"I didn't recognize him at first," one said. "But he sure looks a lot like him, doesn't he?"

"In the car, Reeder. You're coming with us."

55

In Custody

Owen wanted to tell them everything, but surely they'd admit him to an insane asylum. The Valley of Shoam, the Castle of the Pines, Erol's clan, the islands of Mirantha, the White Mountain, a Dragon, the King? Uh-huh.

"I was on a trip," Owen said.

The radio squawked something about an attack.

"Buckle up, kid. We need to take this call."

They raced down a residential street and into a subdivision of nice houses with rolling green lawns, passed a soccer field, and pulled up to a house.

The officers left Owen locked in

the back and separated from his sword and the front seat by a shield of Plexiglas. There were no handles on the inside of the back doors. He was trapped.

A woman in a bathrobe stumbled onto the porch crying and pointing, and the officers followed her inside.

A child on a bike slowed, looking at Owen.

Owen pounded on the window. "Let me out of here! I have to get home! Please open the door!"

The kid stopped and stared blankly, then glanced around and pedaled away quickly. Behind him flew some sort of buzzing, clicking creature, larger than a bee and more like a small bird, though it passed so fast that Owen could not get a good look at it.

When the officers returned, one said, "I've had a lot of weird calls, but this is a first. Bee sting. Can you believe it?"

"Looked pretty nasty," the other said. "More like a bite than a sting, but what do I know? Maybe it's a rabid bee."

Owen leaned forward. "I saw something pass the car while you guys were inside—"

"Sit back, kid! You're in enough trouble as it is."

"Trouble? What have I done?"

"Your old man is in a lot of trouble. And if I were you, I'd try giving a straight story instead of the stuff he's been dishing out about coming from some other dimension, that he wasn't really your dad and was only supposed to watch you and make sure you didn't get away."

The second officer turned. "He's been charged with your murder, trial to begin next week. Your showing up will put a little crimp in that case."

A few minutes later the officers paraded Owen before the chief of police, a balding man with a white mustache and coffee-stained teeth. He studied Owen like a specimen on a slide. "Sure looks like him. Guess we won't know for sure until we do a DNA match with that crazy old bird who claims he's been keeping the boy away from the Dragon."

"What?" Owen said, sitting up.

"Well, it talks," the chief said. "Would you mind telling us where you've been the past few weeks?"

"Glad to," Owen said. "But first I want to talk with my father."

"So he is your father?" the man said. "Set them up in inter-rogation three."

Owen had seen enough police
shows to know the officers were
behind the big window in the wall,
watching and listening to every word.
But he didn't care. He also knew from
The Book of the King that his return to
the Highlands had a higher purpose.
But what?

He whispered, "'The hands of the
King hold the heart of his Son. The
King directs it like a channel of water
and makes it go where he pleases.
Everyone thinks they know which way
to go, but the King looks deep into the
heart.'"

Through his shirt Owen patted

Mucker, now shrunk to his original size. "Rest, my friend. You did well to get us here."

Owen's father wore handcuffs and looked tired and older than when Owen had last seen him. He sat heavily as his escorting officer stepped out.

"You're back," Mr. Reeder said. "How were your travels?"

"Interesting. Dangerous. More exciting than I could ever have imagined."

A hint of a smile broke on the man's face. "Did you use the pictures I gave you?"

"I found the woman. I returned her son to her."

Mr. Reeder sat bolt upright. "From the White Mountain? What do you mean you returned him?"

"He's safe and back with his mother. But clouds gather on the Lowlands. There will be an attack." Owen licked his chapped lips, his mouth dry. He whispered, "Why did you pretend to be what you were not?"

"It was the only way I knew to get my son back," Mr. Reeder said.

Owen's mind flashed to the blond-haired boy in the cavern, his mother in Yuhrmer, and the frozen arm sticking out of the mountain. "But I found the boy's father on the mountain. Dead."

"There are things you still do not know," Mr. Reeder said, "even after reading the book." He searched Owen's face, as if trying to communicate something without speaking. "There are shadows here and echoes of this place in the Lowlands."

"What do you mean?"

Someone screamed down the hall. Owen heard chairs slide on the floor behind the window and people running.

"The minions have been loosed," Mr. Reeder said.

"Minions?"

"Get me out of here and I'll tell you everything."

Could Owen trust this man? He had lived with him as his son for years. How could Mr. Reeder have kept the truth from him for so long? Maybe because his real son's life depended on it.

Owen ran to the door and peeked out. Everyone had raced to the screams echoing down the hallway.

"They're inside!" a man said. "Hundreds of 'em! Get in an office and shut the door!"

Owen shut the door and looked pleadingly at Mr. Reeder.

"I told you," the man said. "The minions have been here for days. They're the Dragon's special creation—

part bee, part lion, and part venomous snake. They inject venom into humans that makes them age quickly. Enough venom and the human can die. Otherwise a drop can age a person many years."

"Why would he unleash them here in the Highlands?"

"Who knows the mind of the Dragon or why he does what he does? I despaired of ever getting back to my family, and once you left, I knew my son was doomed."

"You are from Yuhrmer. You worked for the blacksmith there."

Mr. Reeder's eyes narrowed. "Why do you think this?"

"Your wife is the baker Drushka. She gave us bread for our journey. But why didn't she recognize your picture?"

"Who is 'we'?"

"A Watcher was my constant companion in the Lowlands. And a horse."

"Do you have a weapon?" the man said.

Owen told him of the Sword of the Wormling and that the officers had confiscated it.

"Then it is true. That is your identity."

Owen nodded. "I won't leave here without it. Now tell me, is your wife the baker?"

"In a way, yes. I would explain, but we are out of time."

Something hit the window in the door, and the man recoiled. Owen studied the face of the creature, ignoring

the horror in favor of his overwhelming curiosity. Its eyes
bugged out but looked human. The sharp teeth covered
a slithering tongue, and its wings were golden brown and
leathery. It had four legs with sharp spines and something
that looked like sharpened metal on the end. It growled at
Owen and made a squeaking sound that brought other minions to the door.

There was no other exit, so Owen flicked off the light and
ordered Mr. Reeder to sit with his back to the door.

"If they don't see or hear us," Owen whispered, "maybe
they'll lose interest."

The two settled into a long silence, broken only by the
beasts trying to burrow under the door. Owen took off his
shirt and stuffed it underneath.

"Why did you keep me cooped up in that bookstore for so
long?" Owen finally whispered.

"Obeying orders. I was told to keep your identity from you."

"What identity is that?"

"I was told you were special and that someone would come
looking for you. If I fulfilled my task until your 18th birthday,
I would be reunited with my wife and child. Shortly before
you left I discovered you were the Wormling."

"And you believed that? Was it the Dragon who talked you
into this?"

"One of his henchmen told me I could obey or die, simple as that."

"You failed," Owen said. "Why haven't you been killed?"

"All in good time, my friend. Perhaps the minions are my punishment."

Owen put his head back and leaned against the door. "How could you be the husband of Drushka without her recognizing your picture?"

Mr. Reeder took a deep breath. "This is how it was explained to me." He pointed to his palm. "This side of your hand is what you use to grasp things—a pencil, a book, pages. It is vital to dexterity." He turned his hand over. "This side merely mirrors the movements of the other side. But the two are not two at all but one."

"I understand, but what does that have to do with—?"

"Probably something in the book explains it."

"Many parts of the book I don't understand, but I don't remember anything that talks of hands and—"

"Not hands but worlds. Doesn't it say anything about the two worlds being united?"

Owen gasped. "Of course! The book says when the Son returns he will defeat the Dragon and unite the two worlds with his marriage."

"There you are."

"But that doesn't explain how you could be here and in the

Lowlands and have a wife who doesn't even recognize your picture."

Mr. Reeder sighed heavily. Then he stood and looked out the window. "I think they're gone," he said, handing Owen his shirt. "Let's get your sword."

When Owen opened the door, the buzzing sounded muffled behind him. He raced to the front of the station, Mr. Reeder close at his heels, to the desk of the officer who had taken his sword. It wasn't there, but he found a key ring with a tiny key that removed Mr. Reeder's handcuffs.

"They're coming," Mr. Reeder hissed. "The minions know you're here."

"Help me find the sword," Owen said, fear creeping into his voice.

Owen tore through the halls, looking under desks and through windows into locked offices.

Mr. Reeder gave a halfhearted effort, more interested, it seemed, in finding a place to hide.

Toward the rear of the front section was an office with Evidence Room over the door. The window and door were covered with wire mesh, but Owen could see the sword atop the long counter inside. The door was, of course, locked.

Buzzing and clicking raised the hair on Owen's neck. Mr. Reeder said something, but Owen paid no attention. He flew back for the key ring and tried every key as fast as he could.

"We've got to go!" Mr. Reeder said.

Finally one worked, and Owen was in.

"No!" Mr. Reeder shouted, backing into a corner. "Stay away from me!"

Owen grabbed the sword, instantly feeling power surge through him. He returned to where Mr. Reeder waved at one of the beasts.

"Leave him alone!" Owen yelled.

The minion turned and locked eyes with Owen, then threw back its head and gave an otherworldly screech that seemed to summon all its friends.

"What are you doing here, Wormling?" the high-pitched voice said. "Why have you come to torment us?"

So the sword allowed him to understand the buzzing language!

"To send you back where you've come from," Owen said. "Leave here or die."

"We have work to do," the minion growled. "We search for the girl at the Dragon's behest."

A fire raged in Owen's chest, and he lunged at the creature with such force and speed that it was sliced in two, its halves quivering on the floor, wings flapping pathetically.

"Were you stung?" Owen said.

Mr. Reeder shook his head. "You have become strong."

Owen helped him up, but as they reached the door a swarm of beasts hit the glass, screaming, "Get the Wormling!"

A screeching voice, lower than the others, bellowed over the noise, "We've found the girl! Follow me!"

Most of the swarm left, following the larger minion that appeared to be wearing armor.

Owen's mind raced. *What girl? And where?*

Owen sprinted to the door. "Are you coming?"

"Out there?" Mr. Reeder said. "You have to be crazy."

"It's our only chance."

The man pulled his knees to his chest and rocked like a child. "I can't."

Owen plunged out the door, the minions clanging off his sword with each swing. He was sure a few minions got through before the door shut, because of Mr. Reeder's screams.

Owen discovered that simply holding the sword in front

of him as he ran both attracted and warded off his attack-
ers. They flew headlong into it—as metal is drawn toward a
magnet.

He caught the swarm of minions and their commander two
blocks ahead after he ran through an alley and crossed a park-
ing lot. The leader was so large it could fly only a few feet off
the ground, and the others swarmed around it.

The farther Owen ran, the more familiar the streets looked.
There was the grocery and the library and a row of houses
that stood like sentinels. The streets were deserted, and Owen
noticed a child in a second-floor window watching with
astonishment before being whisked away by someone.

He stayed about a half block behind the swarm, many minions still clanking off his sword. Clouds covered the sky, and
a dark patch against the mountains lit with lightning. Owen
ran on, remembering from *The Book of the King*:

> Do not toss away your belief in the King; that assurance
> will be rewarded. Keep going, no matter how difficult
> the road, so that when you have followed all the King's
> directions, you will see his words come to pass.

"She's in there!" the minion commander yelled. "Get her."

Owen turned the corner to see the familiar glow from the
front windows of the Briarwood Café. People at tables looked
in openmouthed horror at the oncoming horde. One man ran

outside, only to be quickly overcome by the minions until he lay motionless on the ground.

Owen dropped to his knees when he saw Clara Secrest at the counter.

The commander saw her too. "That's her! That's the girl!"

59

Her

Simply a young girl with a good heart and a pretty face to this point in our story and having seen her listen to and counsel Owen the last time he was in the Highlands, we now take a closer look at Clara Secrest. That she carries so many plates on one arm and has made sure each order is correct (no cheese on the spinach salad, no mayonnaise on the chicken sandwich) tells us what a hard worker she is and that she cares about details. Her kindness toward children becomes obvious when she kneels beside a young boy who's struggling through his order. She smiles and looks him straight in the eye.

It appears a normal evening at the restaurant, with the usual number of people there for their senior citizens' discount as well as the raucous high school crowd. Four boys wearing baseball hats low on their foreheads sit in the back and laugh louder than the rest of the room combined, but they don't seem to care.

One watches Clara, and she feels his eyes as she works her tables. She ignores the boys' chuckles and loud references to her, another positive trait of this young girl.

But the mood changes quickly, and customers drop their forks and point at the oncoming swarm of—what? Bees? Too big to be bees. More like small birds with big teeth and piercing eyes. And they look hungry.

When the creatures smack the front windows, Clara drops plates and people jump and run for the back. Screams fill the dining room, which makes the owner rush out.

"What's all the noise?" he yells, glaring at Clara and apparently ready to holler at her for dropping the food.

Clara points a shaky finger at the front window, and the owner is suddenly speechless. He moves out from behind the counter, wiping his hands on his apron and squinting. "What in the world are those things?"

When the big one squeals in some incomprehensible language, the owner takes a step back. His look is the same as if someone had pulled a dead rat from one of his dinners. He walks to the windows and pulls the blinds. But the beasts keep ramming the windows, screaming and gnashing their teeth.

"What do they want?" an older woman shouts.

"Calm down," the man whispers, turning off the lights and scurrying to the back.

A child weeps uncontrollably, nearly breaking Clara's heart. She has a tender spot for all children, perhaps because she feels lost and alone like many of them.

She kneels next to two frightened children. "It's okay. We're safe in here." Their parents seem occupied with their own fear.

One of the raucous boys taps Clara on the shoulder. She can smell the onions on his breath and knows it's Gordan, because he was the only one who ordered onion rings.

"Sit with us if those things scare you," Gordan says.

She wants to say, "I wouldn't sit with you if your booth was the last safe place on earth," but because she has a good heart and knows they would only laugh more, she simply smiles and turns back to the children.

With the blinds pulled, no one can see the beasts clicking and clacking to get inside. However, a few of the creatures have come to the side windows. Something about them triggers a memory—or perhaps a nightmare Clara has had—and she presses her temples.

The dream is of fire and sharp talons. She is young and

being taken from everything she has known and loved. Down the hall she hears her parents screaming. Through the massive dark stone hallways she is pulled, grasped tightly, hair flying. And suddenly she is flying through the frigid wind with nothing but her nightclothes and her favorite blanket.

The teen boys abandon their booth and move into the bathroom, closing the door on others who bang and try to push their way in.

Suddenly the glass at the front of the restaurant gives a sickening crack. It won't be long before the creatures break through. Clara huddles with the others, unable to tear her eyes from the window.

Then a light shines outside and penetrates the shades as it approaches. Clara kneels with the children as the light grows brighter. The clicking and screeching of voices lessen, as if they had been called to another battle. The cracking of the window is replaced by a soft pinging, like marbles hitting a suit of armor.

It is deathly quiet inside, besides the gasping of adults and the whimpering of children. The pinging stops outside, and the light goes out.

A girl looks up at Clara with doe eyes. "Is it over?" she says, voice shaking.

Clara whispers, "I hope so."

The doorknob turns. Children gasp. A woman clutches her

husband's arm. The owner grabs a steak knife from a table and brandishes it, though whoever is at the door cannot see him.

As the door opens, Clara can see little until a sliver of light flashes and the orange glow of the kitchen stove reflects off something metallic.

"Hello?" a male voice says softly, then more manly and urgently, "You people still in here?"

"What do you want?" the owner says.

"You need to get out," the young man says. "The minions are down for the moment, but that won't last."

Something about the voice stirs Clara, jogs her memory. "Owen!" she says and rushes to him.

"Clara, stay away from him!" the owner yells. "He has a weapon!"

"I know him. He's my friend." She turns to Owen. "Where have you been? Everyone's been looking for you."

The others begin crowding around, even the bathrooms emptying. Someone says, "What did you call those things?"

"Minions. And they're down only temporarily. If you live near here, go. If not, find a safe spot and stay."

Gordan calls out, "Well, if it isn't the invisible freshman. Where have you been?"

Clara is fascinated by the change in Owen's demeanor, by the way he stands straighter, chest out. His muscles are bigger, and he seems to look straight through Gordan. When she last saw Owen, his fear of Gordan and the others was palpable. Now he is anything but afraid. *What has happened to my friend?*

Owen looks past Gordan. "Whoever wants to leave should do so now. Otherwise you'll be trapped here until the attack is over."

"Who died and put you in charge?" Gordan says. "And where'd you get that thing?" He looks back at his friends. "Don't get too close or he'll use his new rubber sword."

Owen opens the door. "Leave now. This will be your only chance."

A few walk out, but most stay.

Gordan grabs Owen by the shirt as he passes. "We have a score to settle, kid."

Owen grips Gordan's hand, and Clara marvels at how Owen has grown. Gordan used to seem so much bigger, but now they're almost eye to eye.

Gordan grimaces and lets go of Owen's shirt as the two lock eyes.

"I agree," Owen says, "but now is not the time."

"Be careful," Gordan says, flexing his hand. "Threats can come back to haunt you." He walks out, his friends close behind.

Owen pulls Clara outside. "We need to talk."

He draws his sword at a buzzing in the distance, and Clara

steps over writhing and squirming minions. "They're coming back to life."

"We have a little time," Owen says. "You live nearby, don't you?"

Clara nods. "I'll show you."

60

Talking

Owen felt a new strength as he
walked Clara through the old
streets. Still, something about coming
back made Owen feel small again. He
had been through so much and learned
even more, but now he was treated like
his old self—not royalty but rabble.

A new wave of minions flew in as
he and Clara reached her house. Owen
pushed her behind him as he raised his
sword.

"He's found the girl!" a minion shouted, and the news echoed
throughout the horde. "The Dragon
will not like it! Attack!"

But as they dived toward him, one
by one they were drawn into his sword
like moths to a flame.

When the onslaught was over, the pile of minions was up to their ankles.

"How did you learn to do that?"

Owen took her hand. "Come inside. I have a lot to tell you."

Clara's parents were not at home. Owen went through the house making sure the windows were closed and there was no way the minions could get in.

He wondered what the minions had meant calling Clara "the girl." And at the restaurant the minion commander had referred to her the same way. A shudder ran through him. Could Clara be his bride? And if so, how would he explain? How could he even begin to tell her all that had happened?

Securing the windows in her room, he saw a nicely made bed and two waitress uniforms among the clothes in her closet.

Owen paused at her small desk, where she had written on a tablet:

> I fear change, but I know I cannot grow without it. And it seems a great change is coming. The darkness encroaches. I feel it seeping in every day. I've tried to talk with Mom and Dad about it, but they do not have the same feeling. Or perhaps they do not want to admit it.

Owen tore his eyes from the page. He felt guilty reading her thoughts, yet something drew him. Some connection—something familiar.

Where do I start? Will she believe any of it?

The teakettle whistled, and Owen hurried down to where Clara had set out two cups for them.

"So where have you been?" Clara said. "Your father has been accused of terrible things. We even did an article about you in the school newspaper."

"Who wrote it?"

"I did." She retrieved a paper from a stack in the corner. On the front was his picture—his hair frighteningly out of place and a huge red zit on his chin.

> *No News of Missing Student*
>
> The disappearance of Owen Reeder has students, faculty, and the administration concerned. Authorities are investigating the events leading to his vanishing, but police admit they have few leads.

The story went on to quote friends and acquaintances, including Owen's teachers. One name caught his attention.

> *Mrs. Rothem, one of Reeder's former teachers, was reassigned to another school shortly before Reeder went missing.*

She says he was one of her favorite students.

"Owen is unique," she says. "He has such strength and power of mind. I've seen that kind of intellect only a few times, and it usually consumes the person. They become puffed up because of it. But there is a great humility in Owen, and I don't doubt that he'll go far. I just worry that something terrible has happened and that we'll never know how great he can be."

"How did you find her?" Owen said, taking a sip of tea.

"It wasn't easy, but what good thing is?"

"Where did you hear that?" Owen said, his heart racing.

"From Mrs. Rothem. She said I should keep searching. That one day you would return. She asked me not to put it in my story, but she talked as if she knew you'd return at the right time. What she didn't say was where you went. She didn't know."

"If I told you, you wouldn't believe me."

"Try me."

Owen took a deep breath. "I used to think this was the only world—that there was nothing other than us."

Clara squinted. "You haven't been abducted by aliens, have you?"

Owen laughed. "In some ways I wish I was. No, there is more than you can imagine out there, another world much like ours and yet so different. There is also unspeakable evil there."

"Like here. A hideous man has been watching the restaurant. The police chased him off once. He just stands and watches."

"What does he look like?" Owen said, setting down his teacup.

"He's tall, but he stays in the shadows. One of our customers says he has severe burn scars on his face and neck."

"It's him," Owen whispered. "He didn't die after all."

"Who?" Clara said.

"He's talking about your enemy," a voice said behind them. Owen turned to see a man and a woman.

"It's him," the woman said.

61

Twin Identities

O n your feet," the man said. He clearly held a weapon of some sort beneath his long coat.

"Dad," Clara said, "this is my friend. Don't hurt him."

"He is no friend of yours or ours," the woman said. "He means to destroy what we've worked to preserve."

Standing straight and staring at the woman, Owen fought the old, familiar feeling of smallness. "I've not come to destroy anything but the enemy. And I have no thoughts but safety for Clara."

"What have you tried to preserve, Mom?" Clara said.

The woman looked pityingly at

Clara, and Owen wondered if this was the way a real mother would treat her child.

"Don't you understand?" the woman said. "This one was sent to herald the coming of the new system. And if that is true, we lose everything."

"What could you possibly lose if the true King is on his throne?" Owen said.

The man sneered. "Our daughter. She is to be returned to us."

"Returned?" Clara said.

"We can't possibly explain," he snapped. "You must trust us."

Owen ran a hand through his hair, searching for words. "Clara, the other world I spoke of . . . I believe it is a mirror of sorts. I don't understand it all yet, but these are not your real parents."

"Of course they are! I've grown up with them."

"Get away from her!" the man said, revealing a gun.

Owen pulled the sword from his belt.

"That won't help you," the man said.

"It's protected me from them," Owen said, nodding toward the back door. Minions circled the window, peering in. "Clara, do you have any childhood memories of being taken away in the night, snatched by some being? Anything like that?"

She looked astonished. "I have had dreams, nightmares—"

"Don't listen to him!" the woman said. "We are your parents, and we have sworn to protect you. Don't let this scoundrel fill your head with nonsense."

"What were the dreams about, Clara?" Owen said.

"I remember fire and terrible eyes." A tear coursed down her cheek. "I thought it was simply a bad dream. I thought . . ." Owen could tell she had moved to a new realization. "But that really happened, didn't it?"

Owen nodded. "You were taken from the other world. The Lowlands."

"Preposterous!" the man shouted.

"Shoot him!" the woman said.

"For what purpose?" Clara said, her eyes locked on Owen's.

"For a destiny you do not yet know," Owen said, voice trembling. "You are Clara in this world, but in the other—"

An explosion rocked the room.

The man moved like a phantom, seemingly unconcerned about the minions, coat flowing with the windstorm that brewed overhead. Why did the minions not attack him? Did they somehow sense his true identity?

At first glance, this man looked like a lonely street person, a vagabond in search of a meal. But upon closer examination, a child could discern from the fiery eyes that something bigger, something much more important drew him.

The man peered into the dimly lit dining room of the Briarwood Café, deliberately scanning the faces. Like a child passing over certain colors of jelly beans, he moved away. Did he not care for those inside? Did this scar-faced, coldhearted man just leave people to their fate?

He turned down Clara Secrest's street as if he'd been there many times. He moved to the back and peeked into the small kitchen window just in time to see a flash and hear a loud pop.

Clara screamed as he rushed in behind the man and woman, knocked the gun from the man's hand, and kicked it away.

Still holding his glowing sword before him, Owen had somehow suspended the bullet in midair a foot off the ground.

The man couldn't help but smile. Owen had grown into quite a young man since he had last seen him, since he had passed along *The Book of the King*.

"Good work," the man said.

63

The Meeting

Owen slowly lowered the sword, and the bullet hit the tile with a clink and rolled.

"You've learned to use the sword well," the strange man said. It was Mr. Page.

"I thought you were dead," Owen whispered.

The man gave a wry smile. "The news of my passing was greatly exaggerated." He looked at Clara. "I hope I didn't frighten you at the restaurant."

"Get out of our house," the woman spat.

Mr. Page faced the couple. "You have done a worthy job of protecting the girl," he said, plainly working to control some emotion deep within. "However, your job is complete. I will care for her now."

"You?" the woman said. "By what authority? She doesn't want anything to do with someone so hideous."

Mr. Page drew closer, and the woman shrank back. "First, she is not your daughter. You've known that all along. Second, I will not take orders from you. I have her best interests at heart and will see that she fulfills her destiny."

"Destiny?" Clara said.

"All in good time," Mr. Page said. "Let me get you to safety, and then we will discuss your future."

A buzzing sounded behind them as two minions streaked through the open door and attacked the man and woman, biting their necks.

Mr. Page knocked the minions to the floor, swept them from the room, and closed the door. He grabbed Clara's hand. "We must hurry."

Owen stood openmouthed until Mr. Page looked back. "Are you coming?"

"In a moment," he said.

The woman screamed as Owen lowered his sword onto her neck. The man snarled and reached, trying to stop Owen. But Owen gently placed the blade against her skin, immediately healing the bite wound. He did the same for the man.

"You will receive your child back at the right time," Mr. Page said. He turned to Clara and Owen. "Now come. Time is short."

Clara hesitated, eyes downcast. She looked back at her parents.

"Come, child," Mr. Page said softly.

Owen held his sword high as Clara huddled between him and Mr. Page. They hurried into the night, and the minions screeched overhead.

"What are they saying?" Clara said.

"That he has found both of us," Owen said. "That the Dragon will be furious."

"Dragon?" Clara said.

"The enemy of us all," Mr. Page said. "The one who sent these beasts."

"And caused the scars on your face?" Clara said.

"A small price. Soon the Dragon will be defeated but not without a terrible fight," Mr. Page said. "Follow me."

Owen was kept busy protecting Clara from diving minions. He stunned them with his sword, and then Mr. Page tossed them aside.

They walked until the streets ended and they were on dirt and grass. In the woods at the edge of the mountain they came upon a deserted shack in good enough condition to keep the minions out.

A passage from *The Book of the King* came back to Owen, and he said:

> "For though he is high and lofty, yet will he make his home with the poor. Like a beggar he will dwell with a humble spirit, so that he might revive the hearts of those who need forgiveness."

Mr. Page looked back at Owen. "Go on. Say the rest." Owen tried to remember, but his mind was blank. Mr. Page said:

> "It is for the sick he has come. And the needy. And the downtrodden. And all those whose hearts did once burn within them, who are now but shadows of what will be."

"You memorized it?" Owen said. "Before you brought it from the King, you memorized the entire book?"

The Dragon's commanders, along with their lead warriors, assembled before the Dragon's lair. The line stretched the entire length of the castle at least 50 deep. Each pair represented a thousand troops assembled in the valley beyond the castle. Campfires had been doused, and each fighter stood at attention, waiting for the signal to attack.

The Dragon rubbed his claws and watched from a window, waiting for just the right moment to make his appearance. He was sure this would be his finest hour.

When all were in place and had saluted the castle, the Dragon cleared his throat and sent a blast of fire through an opening in the stone tower, lighting the sky.

Cheers from the commanders were overwhelmed by the shouts from the sea of warriors and the screeching of demon flyers.

The Dragon drank in the crescendo, and when he appeared through the high-arched gate, the mob roared anew.

"Quite an entrance, sire," RHM said. "You deserve this."

"Yes," the Dragon purred. "They do know greatness when they see it, don't they?"

The cacophony continued until the Dragon hovered above the castle, then settled on the parapet where everyone could see him.

"My kingdom will be forever!" the Dragon said.

The crowds went wild again.

"The days of the Wormling are over, and his servants who remain must be utterly destroyed. They have broken their treaty and swear allegiance to another. They will be crushed."

The Dragon launched another prolonged blast while the troops screamed and thrust their weapons in the air. His eyes burned red, and he licked his charred teeth as if devouring his dinner.

"Unleash my power and my vengeance!" he howled. "Leave no one alive. Wipe them from this world so that we might replenish it anew!"

Back in his lair at the top of the castle, blood still boiling from his own rousing speech, the Dragon was interrupted by RHM ushering in a smallish demon flyer.

"News from the Highlands, sire."

"I know," the Dragon said, cackling. "The minions have done their work. We'll soon have both worlds to ourselves."

The small creature waddled forward, eyes focused on the floor. He stopped 10 yards from the Dragon and bowed. "I was flying by the w-w-wood, sire, away from the town. And I n-noticed a group walking there."

"Unstung?"

"Apparently, sire. An older man with a long coat. Scars on his face and neck. And a boy with a long sword."

The Dragon drew close, his nose nearly touching the small flyer, who closed his eyes and seemed prepared to be incinerated. "Two is not a group."

"Quite right, s-sire. A girl was with them. They were protecting her from the minions. Between the sword and the old man's scarred hands, they just fell away. I've never seen anything like it."

The Dragon whimpered like a small woodland animal, something flickering through his mind. Could his enemy have survived his fiery blast on the hill in the Highlands? Could he be joining forces with the Wormling, showing him the location of the Son? He turned to the quavering being in front of him. "Did they hear you, know you were there?"

"I don't think so, s-sire. I came as fast as I could to tell you the news."

The Dragon gazed out at the armies marching to battle. "This is not bad news—not at all. The enemy is constrained. The Wormling will not have time to finish breaching the portals before his precious friends die."

The Dragon's ears pricked as a tiny puff floated across the wind. Two wings. Smallish wings unaccustomed to this altitude.

No matter. Whoever it was would be killed before the day was out.

65

Mr. Page

Owen followed Mr. Page and Clara inside the small shack, where a candle burned on the table near a loaf of bread and a jug of juice. Mr. Page ate like a hungry wolf. Logs burned in the fireplace, and his eyes sparkled as he ate. He finally excused himself and went into a bedroom with a blanket covering the doorway.

"What is he going to do?" Clara said. "Where is he taking us?"

"We can trust this man. He gave me *The Book of the King*." Owen showed it to Clara, and she began to read it. The same thing that had happened to him when he first saw the words was apparently happening to her. She couldn't tear herself from the book.

Mr. Page returned, looking haggard. While Clara read, he took Owen to the fire and sat on the floor beside him.

"There is not much time," Mr. Page said. "Any questions about what you are to do?"

Owen stared. "I have nothing but questions. I have no idea what to do."

"But you know who you are."

"Yes," he said, lowering his voice.

Mr. Page smiled and clapped a hand behind Owen's neck. "Then you know what to do."

"I know I am to defeat the Dragon and marry the princess, and somehow that union will change things in both the Highlands and the Lowlands. But I don't know who the princess is or how this will all take place."

"Doesn't the book say something about its being a light for your course?"

"'The King's words are a light for my pathway, a sure guide for every step I take.'"

Mr. Page smiled. "You doubt those words?"

"I do not, but there are so many decisions to make. I don't know which words to follow."

"Follow all of them with your whole heart. Do not try to separate one from another. They are a unit."

"But isn't there something missing—something that needs to be completed?"

Mr. Page stoked the fire. "The keeper of the fire makes sure it does not go out, no matter how cold the night becomes. And you must tend the fire of your heart, brave Owen."

"I'm not sure I know what you mean."

"Things ahead will threaten to undo you, may make it appear as if everything you've learned and have been fighting for has been for nothing. Do not give in to those thoughts."

Owen nodded, still unsure.

"Your fight is not against flesh and blood but against the powers of darkness that seek to cover the land. Your fight begins here—" he pointed to Owen's chest—"and ends here." He pointed to his head.

"I've struggled greatly," Owen said. "I've fought beasts I never could have imagined."

"And you have struggled well. That is all the King asks of you. You have the heart of a warrior, the heart of your father. But you also have the heart of a poet." Mr. Page held out both his hands. "You are both warrior and poet. The Highlands and the Lowlands are lands of warriors and poets. Fighters and singers. Understand?"

"Mirrors," Owen said, closing his eyes and remembering the faces of Erol and Watcher and Mordecai. "Beings there seem similar to people I know here. A friend there is a

Watcher who senses things and protects me. She also talks like a waterfall, and I could drown in her words. But she seems very much like a friend here named Constance—I call her Connie. You met her after you gave me the book. Beneath the B and B."

Mr. Page smiled sadly. "I know her well. That's where I found her not long ago—near the minions' nest. I've been watching her since you were gone. And Clara too."

"You said something to Constance the day you left, the day I thought you died. What was it?"

"She will tell you. Just remember that things are not always as they seem, Owen. 'Those who die shall live again. Those who are weak shall become strong. Those who recognize their faults shall become faultless.' But not on their own. Only through the King's power. Understand?"

"I understand that I don't understand."

The man chuckled. "'The blind shall see. The deaf shall hear. The valleys will rise and the mountains be brought low.' What awaits you, dear Owen, is too much for me to even begin to describe. But I must ask you something."

"Anything."

Mr. Page nodded to Clara. "Who do you think she is?"

She seemed to scan the words in *The Book of the King* as if they were pieces of gold. Her face and hair glowed in the firelight.

"I'm afraid to say," Owen whispered.

"Then let me tell you," Mr. Page said. "She was taken when she was young, just a few years older than you. Her mother and I have missed her terribly." He bit his lip. "She is my beloved daughter."

The room seemed to grow smaller, as if Owen and Mr. Page were the only two in it. "Is she to be my wife?"

The skin around Mr. Page's eyes crinkled. "A sister is born to stick by her brother to the end. And she will do this. Clara is your sister. But the woman you are betrothed to lies in there."

The words struck Owen's heart like an arrow. "Clara is my sister?"

The man nodded.

Owen could hardly breathe, his mind swirling in some familial equation that seemed to make sense. "And if you are her father and I am her brother, then you are *my* father. You are the King. . . ."

Mr. Page hugged Owen tight and whispered, "I told you things are not always as they seem." He pulled back, tears in his eyes. "How I've longed to hold you, my Son, longed to tell you how much I love you and how long I have searched."

"Father," Owen choked, burying his head in the man's chest.

Watcher returned to find a dis-
pute over who would be the
leader of the army now. Everyone
knew there was no way the Wormling
could have survived the onslaught of
the Dragon.

"Mordecai should lead us," Erol said.
"He was the Wormling's teacher and
friend."

"But he left Connor in charge,"
someone else said.

Others weighed in, saying it didn't
matter, that without the Wormling
they were doomed.

But a deep voice cut through the
din. "The Wormling is not dead! He
will return as he said!" It was Rogers,
the young lad the Wormling had taken

under his wing. "He promised I would be at his side when he fought the battle, and that's where I'm going to be!"

The whole camp quieted. Many of the older ones of Erol's clan began a dirge for the Wormling, a sad song that made everyone listen.

Watcher went to Connor, then to Mordecai, and all gathered around and pleaded with them to stay together and wait for word from the Wormling.

"The only word we are going to get now is the call of the war horn," Connor said. "They will descend and tear us to pieces if we don't prepare to fight."

"But the Wormling said—"

"Your Wormling is dead. Can't you understand that? I wish it weren't true, but if there's anything he taught us, it was to discover the truth and believe it."

"But he said he would return. He wanted me to convince you of that and not to fight prematurely."

Connor knelt and looked Watcher in the eye. "There is no future for us here. There is no future for us, period. We will fight and we will die. But at least we will have fought."

The group took shelter in the forest of Emul, under the leafy trees, but at nightfall came a stiff wind, and the leaves scattered like frightened birds.

Watcher had lost her power to sense an invisible invasion, but something told her evil was on its way.

Spellbound

Owen's father ushered him to the doorway of the bedroom.

"I found my mother," Owen whispered. "The Queen. But I did not know she was my mother. Now she is lost."

"You will find her. You must find her."

"But won't the Dragon pour out his wrath on her?"

"The Dragon will do as he wills. That does not change my plan. Be careful when you return to the Lowlands."

"I know I must go back to breach the four portals and fulfill the prophecy. But I have breached only two of them. So I must go back twice?"

"You must understand why the portals are there to begin with. I made them. I provided them as a way to bring both worlds together, but they were sealed by the Dragon and the earth was moved inside. Until you, the only way to the Highlands was through the heavenly realm."

"The Dragon made those seals with his likeness and put them there?"

"Yes."

"But you breached the portal under the bookstore."

"True, but the Dragon blocked it again. The only way for the path to be opened was for you to move through with the help of Mucker. You are one of them—the Highlanders and Lowlanders. You are my Son, but you are also one of them. Do you understand?"

Owen nodded. "But why would I need to break through all four portals?"

"To release the stronghold of the Dragon. Because you moved through those portals, you have gained entry for everyone from the Highlands and Lowlands to be united. Their worlds can be joined, and they again can be whole through the power of the words of the book and the power of the King."

Owen thought for a moment. "If I go back to the Lowlands, that's only three portals I've breached. Where's the fourth?"

The King smiled. "Now I will tell you something even the

Dragon does not know. When you return to the Lowlands, you will have breached all four."

"How?"

"Remember I wrote of these portals. They were made by me and only sealed by the Dragon. Three portals joined the earthly kingdoms, but one portal was the realm of the heavenlies. That is the way you were taken when you were young. Do you see?"

Owen's eyes widened. "When he took me from you."

The King's eyes twinkled in the firelight. "I was able to use even the Dragon's snatching of you for my own purposes."

"It is too much to take in," Owen said. "All you've planned is wonderful."

"And the future is more wonderful than you can imagine."

"Will you come with me, Father?"

The King put a hand on Owen's head. "I have work to do. Trust me. I will never leave you. I will never abandon you. Do you believe that?"

Owen nodded. "You have always been with me. Even when I did not know you were looking for me. I felt you through every story, every longing."

"Go to her," the King said. "Speak with your future bride."

Owen pushed the hanging blanket aside and stepped in. Only the flicker of a candle gave light here. The floor creaked beneath Owen as he neared the bed. The covers moved and

Owen's heart fluttered. He had never been so frightened and excited.

Owen heard a groan and saw matted, gray hair and one eye peeking at him.

"Owen? Is that you?"

Owen was sure he had seen those eyes before, but he certainly didn't recognize the voice. Her hair was the color of dirty snow—or was that just the effect of the candle?

"Do I know you?" Owen said.

"For only a short time," the woman said, sitting up so Owen finally saw her entire face. "But I feel like I've known you all my life."

The woman's face was wrinkled and rough from age. She appeared old enough to be Owen's grandmother. The woman sensed his unease. "The man in there brought me to this place after I was bitten."

Owen wished he could heal her with the sword, but he knew it was too late. He knelt and looked into the woman's eyes. There was something familiar there, but he couldn't place it. A sadness covered her face.

A strong wind shook the shack violently, and Owen heard the door open and close. He rose, but the old woman grabbed his arm with a hand gnarled from age. Her body trembled.

"Don't let them bite you," she said, gasping. "The pain is unbearable, and the effect is permanent."

Owen kissed her hand and placed it gently back on the cover. "I will come back for you. We will meet again. Hold on to everything that man tells you."

Owen moved out of the room and back to where Clara continued reading. "Where did Mr. Page go?" he said.

Without looking up she said, "He didn't say."

Though Clara looked as if he were stealing a part of her, Owen closed the book and put it in his pack.

As the wind continued to howl, he nodded toward the bedroom and said, "I need you to watch her. Keep her safe and warm and give her food and water."

"Where will you be?"

"Looking for my father. Our father."

Wielding his sword, Owen ran into the wind, searching the sky for the minions of time. Had they been blown away by the wind?

Darkness gathered thicker than Owen could remember. He ran, searching for any sign of his father, passing the street where the bookstore's sign had fallen at a weird angle and dangled over the sidewalk.

A pack of minions flew overhead, their voices blown about on the wind. Owen strained to hear one exclaim, "He threatens our nest! Converge on him in the power of the Dragon!"

The nest. Under the B and B.

He ran with new purpose and a strength he could not explain. He felt the very picture of the verse in *The Book of the King*:

> The King gives strength to the weary and increases the power of the weak. Even young people grow tired, slip, and fall, but any who put their trust in the King will find new power. They will fly on winged creatures. They will move through the night and not be tired. They will not grow faint, though the task ahead is arduous.

Owen passed the elementary school and neared the burned-out shell of the B and B. A streetlight flickered, and he caught sight of some creature on the side of the blackened building. The end of his sword cast a glow, and he saw it was Mr. Page—the King—his father, scaling the structure.

In a moment Owen would never forget, the man smiled at him, but stubborn and unwavering, he kept climbing until he reached the peak of the only spire left standing. Owen could only look on helplessly, spellbound.

An awful sound behind him made Owen turn to see a group of flying minions, a long mass of gnashing, screeching beasts. Atop the spire, Owen's father opened his coat and tore off his shirt, exposing his chest.

"No!" Owen screamed, throwing his sword as high as he could, but it fell short of the throng of minions.

As the sword descended, the minions screeched and taunted and flew into Owen's father's chest. He wrapped his coat around them as if gathering a stack of unwanted books.

The sword stuck in the earth beside Owen.

His father closed his eyes and fell backward.

Splintering wood was followed by a deep, crushing explosion. Smoke rose from the B and B.

"Oh, Father!"

Batwing flew as fast as his wings would carry him. With every-thing in him he had flown higher than ever—all the way to the Dragon's lair. He saw the Dragon fume and foam and call down curses upon the land. And when the army of the Dragon had moved, so had Batwing. He feared he would be too late to warn Watcher and the others.

Compared to the Dragon's army, the army of the Wormling was small. Batwing knew from talking with the King long before he had even met the Wormling that strength and victory do not come from numbers. But in this case the masses formed against them were simply too overwhelming, and Batwing plunged back to the Lowlands at breakneck speed.

He came near what was left of the White Mountain. Smoke still billowed from it, but there was more smoke in the valley near the forest of Emul. Trees burned, and fields were littered with small, lifeless objects.

Batwing extended his wings, trying desperately to stop, but he crashed into what he thought was a tree stump, only to come to his senses and realize it was one of the clan of Erol.

He fell back, trying to catch his breath, and bumped into another body. Connor stared through lifeless eyes! All around him lay bodies. The land was strewn with the dead. Mordecai lay by a tree, as did Burden.

Batwing stumbled from one body to the next, searching for any sign of the living. When he moved past a large rock and saw four still hooves, he broke down.

"Watcher, I'm sorry!" he sobbed. "I tried to get here to warn you."

He cradled her head in his lap and stared into the distance where the armies of the Dragon retreated. The sorrow nearly broke him.

If only the Wormling were here. If only his sword could touch these friends. If only . . .

Owen grabbed his sword and picked his way through the rubble until he stood over a hole deep in the earth. It had shot straight through the elevator shaft, leaving the space perfectly clean.

He had hoped to find his father and use his sword to heal him. But his father had chosen to take the minions down with him, sacrificing his scarred body.

Owen knelt as sirens blared in the distance. The wind was calm now. A light shone on the horizon as clouds parted.

Owen feared his heart would break, and perhaps it would have had he not heard a whisper. It was the voice he had heard long ago while running from Gordan, the voice he had heard on the mountain. The voice of his friend Nicodemus.

"Remember this, Owen Reeder. You bear the Sword of the Wormling. You are the true Son of the King, the keeper of the sacred book. And the author's blood flows through your veins."

ABOUT THE AUTHORS

Jerry B. Jenkins (jerryjenkins.com) is the writer of the Left Behind series. He owns the Jerry B. Jenkins Christian Writers Guild, an organization dedicated to mentoring aspiring authors. Former vice president for publishing for the Moody Bible Institute of Chicago, he also served many years as editor of *Moody* magazine and now serves on Moody's board of trustees.

His writing has appeared in publications as varied as *Time* magazine, *Reader's Digest, Parade, Guideposts,* in-flight magazines, and dozens of other periodicals. Jenkins's biographies include books with Billy Graham, Hank Aaron, Bill Gaither, Luis Palau, Walter Payton, Orel Hershiser, and Nolan Ryan, among many others. His books appear regularly on the *New York Times, USA Today, Wall Street Journal,* and *Publishers Weekly* best-seller lists.

Jerry is also the writer of the nationally syndicated sports-story comic strip *Gil Thorp*, distributed to newspapers across the United States by Tribune Media Services.

Jerry and his wife, Dianna, live in Colorado and have three grown sons and four grandchildren.

♦♦♦

Chris Fabry is a writer and broadcaster who lives in Colorado. He has written more than 50 books, including the RPM series and collaboration on the Left Behind: The Kids and Red Rock Mysteries series.

You may have heard his voice on Focus on the Family, Moody Broadcasting, or Love Worth Finding. He has also written for *Adventures in Odyssey* and *Radio Theatre*.

Chris is a graduate of the W. Page Pitt School of Journalism at Marshall University in Huntington, West Virginia. He and his wife, Andrea, have nine children, two dogs, and a large car-insurance bill.

RED ROCK MYSTERIES

BRYCE AND ASHLEY TIMBERLINE are normal 13-year-old twins, except for one thing—they discover action-packed mystery wherever they go. Wanting to get to the bottom of any mystery, these twins find themselves on a nonstop search for truth.

CP0140

The Future Is Clear

Check out the exciting Left Behind: The Kids series